Chaimkel
the Dreamer

Chaimkel
the Dreamer

by
Meir Uri Gottesman

CIS
P·U·B·L·I·S·H·E·R·S
New York · London · Jerusalem

A C.I.S. PUBLICATION

Distributed in the U.S., Canada and overseas by
C.I.S. Book Publishers and Distributors
180 Park Avenue, Lakewood, New Jersey 08701
(201) 905-3000 Fax: (201) 367-6666

Distributed in Israel by
C.I.S. International (Israel)
Rechov Hakablan 13/2, Har Nof, Jerusalem
Tel: 02-529-226

Distributed in the U.K. and Europe by
C.I.S. International (U.K.)
1 Palm Court, Queen Elizabeth Walk
London, England N16
Tel: 01-809-3723

Book and Cover Design by Ronda Kruger Israel
Cover and Illustrations by Shepsil Scheinberg
Typography by Chaya Hoberman and Shami Reinman

Printed by Gross Brothers, Inc., Union City, New Jersey

This book is dedicated
to my beloved mother

Rebbitzin Chaya Esther Gottesman עמו״ש

May the Almighty grant her
long and happy years

Table of Contents

Chaimkel
the Dreamer

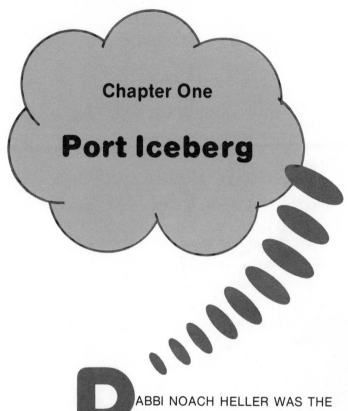

Chapter One

Port Iceberg

RABBI NOACH HELLER WAS THE rabbi of Port Iceberg, Ontario, a remote Canadian town on the shores of Lake Huron where the howling winds were so icy his beard often grew thin icicles when he walked to *shul* on *Shabbos*. Fifty members belonged to the congregation, and each *Shabbos* there were exactly eleven men for the *minyan*.

There was Meir the Tailor, who always fell asleep during the rabbi's sermon. In fact, he secretly planned his whole week around the rabbi's talk. No matter how hard life is, he told himself, I know I will get a good rest when the rabbi talks.

There was Mr. Miller, who owned a dry-goods store. He had lived in Port Iceberg for sixty years. Each *Shabbos* morning, while they waited for the tenth man, he told stories about the First World War, how he had almost been shot in Poland and how he had come to Port Iceberg.

There was Mr. Goldenberg, who owned a department store. He was tall, bald and impatient. There was old Mrs. Goodman, the only woman to attend services. And, of course, there was Mr. Irving Schnitzel, the senior board member.

Each *Shabbos* morning, Rabbi Heller walked to *shul* with his three children. Shulamis, twelve and practical. Chaimkel, ten and dreamy. And Baruch, the four-year-old troublemaker.

Congregation Anshei Iceberg was housed in a large brick building that had been gutted and made into a *shul*. When they reached the *shul*, the rabbi and his children would head straight for the radiator and press their hands and back against the heat. "Florida in Port Iceberg," Rabbi Heller would say.

The rabbi was always the first to arrive. He would quickly open a *Chumash* to study the week's portion, reviewing his *D'var Torah*, the explanation of the reading. He loved the opportunity to learn that came with his job, but he also needed the job to make a living. Indeed, the only skills he had ever seriously developed were studying Torah and being kind to people. Life in

Port Iceberg was difficult, but at least he made a living for his wife and children. All he wanted was to be left alone to serve people and study and teach Torah.

I must stay out of trouble, Rabbi Heller reminded himself each *Shabbos* morning. I must stay away from gossip and *shul* politics.

Shabbos Parshas Shemos, when they began reading the second Book of the Torah, started like any other. It was bitterly cold outside. A bright sun was out, but the lake wind blew mightily, and long, heavy icicles sparkled from every roof. Shulamis, Chaimkel and Baruch played in the *shul* classroom. Hardly anyone was there, except Meir the Tailor, who eagerly awaited the rabbi's sermon.

Like the sun turning in the sky, the regulars showed up at their usual times. Mr. Goldenberg at nine fifteen. Richard Ellis, the social worker, at nine twenty. Mr. Miller, his cheeks pink and his ears bright red like little light bulbs, arrived at nine twenty-five.

"Bingo!" yelled Meir happily, as the tenth man walked in. "We have a *minyan!*"

Rabbi Heller was especially joyful, for each year it thrilled him anew to read of the birth of Moshe. *Shacharis* went well, and by ten thirty, the *Sefer Torah* was taken out from the *Aron Hakodesh.*

Mr. Katz, Port Iceberg's only *Kohain*, was called to the Torah. Mr. Goldenberg, the *Gabbai*, followed closely as Rabbi Heller read from the Torah. A mistake, any mistake, and Mr. Goldenberg swooped down to correct the rabbi in his high-pitched, squeaky voice.

"*Choyos*, not *chayos*!" he interrupted Rabbi Heller, correcting the reading.

Humphh, thought Rabbi Heller, I think I said *choyos*. And he read on.

Rabbi Heller, who was a *Levi,* was called to the second *aliyah*. He kissed the Torah warmly and began to read. Suddenly, he paused. He looked closely at the Torah, and then, he stopped short.

"*Vayelech ish meebais Levi*," said Mr. Goldenberg in an impatient whisper, thinking that the rabbi had lost his place. He was annoyed that Rabbi Heller hadn't prepared properly.

Rabbi Heller just shook his head, not wanting to speak out. He looked at Mr. Goldenberg and then pointed out two words in the scroll. Mr. Goldenberg peered in. Old Mr. Singer, the *Gabbai Sheni*, looked in. Mr. Katz bent over to see what the fuss was about. Meir the Tailor snapped himself awake and ran to see what the fuss was about. The men huddled over the *Sefer Torah*.

"I don't see the problem," declared Mr. Goldenberg, lifting his head.

"What's the matter, Rabbi?" asked Meir respectfully, in his *Litvishe Yiddish*.

Mr. Katz, the *Kohain*, took it more lightly. "I say we go to *Kiddush*," he said. "We'll read it on Sunday."

Rabbi Heller was troubled. He couldn't explain, since doing so would have been an interruption after the *berachah*. He just pointed to the words and shook his head.

"Rabbi, let us proceed," said Mr. Goldenberg, his voice loud and impatient. "It's getting late, and people must get out on time."

The children knew that their father was always nervous when Mr. Goldenberg spoke. The rabbi was turning pale. Chaimkel ran to be near his father.

"Children, away! Children, away!" yelled the *Gabbai Sheni,* who did not know why the rabbi insisted on bringing his children in the first place. But Chaimkel just moved closer to his father, hiding from Mr. Singer's gaze.

Finally, Rabbi Heller lifted his head and rolled the *Sefer Torah* closed. He signalled to Mr. Singer, and the two quickly tied the velvet sash around the *Sefer Torah* and slipped it back into its velvet mantle.

Mr. Goldenberg was furious.

"Rabbi!" he exclaimed. "There is nothing the matter with that *Sefer Torah*! It was donated fifteen years ago by old Mrs. Knuble. Her family will be upset."

But Rabbi Heller did not listen. He returned the *Sefer Torah* to the *Aron Hakodesh* and took out a second, smaller one, with a frayed purple mantle. He opened the smaller *Sefer Torah* to the morning's reading. His voice rising, he began again, *"Vayelech ish . . ."*

Mr. Goldenberg was livid with anger.

Rabbi Heller finished the *aliyah* and recited the second *berachah.*

"Rabbi, you had no right to do that without the permission of the *Gabbai,"* thundered Mr. Goldenberg right in front of the congregation.

"The *Shulchan Aruch* says that a *Sefer Torah* whose letters become rubbed out is *posul*, not kosher," explained Rabbi Heller. "It must be fixed."

"*Shulchan Aruch* or no *Shulchan Aruch*," answered Mr. Goldenberg in a piercing voice. "That's all well enough in Brooklyn where you come from. This is Port Iceberg. All we have is our little congregation, and we can't keep all these extreme laws."

"But it's not extreme," Rabbi Heller protested. "It's—"

Mr. Goldenberg lifted his hand majestically.

"I don't care to debate with you, Rabbi Heller," he said. "You will hear from the Board about this."

Rabbi Heller finished the reading of the *Parshah*, and Meir the Tailor leaned back comfortably to hear the rabbi's sermon. But he was disappointed. The rabbi was so shaken that he couldn't speak. The *minyan* ended quickly, with everyone talking about the same thing, the "big fight *Shabbos* morning at the *shul*."

Chaimkel held on tightly to his father's hand on the long icy walk home. The wind blew little ice-darts into their faces. Usually, on the way home, Rabbi Heller joked and told nice *Shabbos* stories. But that day he walked silently, bent and looking worried. Just before he entered the house, he let out a long sigh.

Poor *Abba*, thought Chaimkel.

By the next morning, all of Port Iceberg's Jewish community knew about the "fist-fight" that almost broke out between the rabbi and Mr. Goldenberg.

Tuesday night, an emergency meeting of the Board

of Directors was held in the *shul* building.

Rabbi Heller was summoned to explain himself. Mr. Goldenberg and the president sat at the head of the table. Mrs. Knuble's two sons, one a doctor, the other an accountant, and her daughter, a tofu distributor, eyed him like the Angel of Death. He felt as though he were on trial for murder.

"Rabbi," intoned Mr. Goldenberg. "The Knuble family demands an apology for your thoughtless action in the *shul* on *Shabbos*."

"But all I did was follow the *Shulchan Aruch*, the Code of Jewish Law," Rabbi Heller explained. "I did what I had to do."

"Rabbi," Mr. Goldenberg answered. "We pay your salary, not some man who wrote the Code. How dare you take such an action without our permission!?"

"But the *Sefer Torah* is not kosher as it is," Rabbi Heller tried to explain. He quickly flipped open a condensed book of Jewish law. "Listen, I had no choice."

Mr. Knuble, the lawyer, jumped up.

"Rabbi, fifteen years before you ever heard of Port Iceberg, my mother scraped up dollar after dollar to pay for that *Sefer Torah*," he shouted. "How dare you tell us it's not kosher?"

Mr. Knuble, the accountant, jumped in after him.

"My grandfather founded this *shul*," he said. "The *Sefer Torah* was donated in his honor. You are insulting my grandfather!"

"But—" Rabbi Heller tried to explain.

"Furthermore, rabbi," interrupted Mr. Goldenberg. "Meir is head of our Ritual and *Kiddush* Committee. Did you consult him before you acted? Meir, did he ask you?"

Meir the Tailor did not answer. He had not heard the question, because he was dozing comfortably. He didn't mean to, but whenever he heard Rabbi Heller's voice he immediately fell asleep.

"But I am the rabbi!" Rabbi Heller finally blurted out without thinking.

The whole Board stared at the rabbi as though he were crazy.

"But it is our *shul*, rabbi," Mr. Goldenberg finally said. "We built it. We were born in Port Iceberg. You came here exactly one and a half years ago. Do you think you are going to tell us what to do?"

"But you don't understand—"

Mr. Robbins, the president of Congregation Anshei Iceberg, finally pounded his gavel gently but firmly. Mr. Robbins owned the largest plant in Port Iceberg, and when he spoke, even the mayor listened.

"Rabbi, I'm sorry, but you're fumbling the ball," said Mr. Robbins. "We have a nice community here. We live in peace with our non-Jewish neighbors. We maintain this building beautifully. We're even putting in a new carpet soon. We all work together, and you're fumbling the ball."

"But—"

"Hear me out, rabbi," continued Mr. Robbins, so sharply that his finely trimmed mustache stood at attention. "We want harmony here. We want peace. We don't need trouble. We like the Knubles. We like their *Sefer Torah*. We don't like anyone from Brooklyn telling Canadians what is kosher and what is not. So, this is what the Board has decided."

Rabbi Heller turned pale.

"Either accept our *Sefer Torah*, our revered *Sefer Torah*, the way it is," continued Mr. Robbins, "or we will consider it a breach of your contract and you will be asked to leave."

"Leave?" asked Rabbi Heller, his voice almost cracking. "Just like that?"

Mr. Robbins smiled icily.

"Peace, rabbi," he said. "*Shalom*. We want peace, friendship and harmony here. Up to now, we haven't complained too loudly about your extreme religious views. But now, you will either cooperate with us, or we will have to bench you."

"Bench me?"

"Yes. Take you out. Send you to the showers."

"To the showers? At forty degrees below zero?"

Meir the Tailor miraculously popped awake.

"Rabbi," he said. "You must understand. Don't make trouble!"

That night, Chaimkel kept his ear close to the wall. He heard his father come in, throw his coat on the couch and sit down with a thud.

Rabbi Heller quickly told his wife everything that happened. His voice grew louder.

"What are we going to do?" he asked. "They are

going to send us away!"

"Don't worry," she answered in a voice so soft Chaimkel almost squeezed off his ear, he pressed so hard to hear. "Hashem will help. It will be all right."

The next day was sad in the Heller household. Rabbi Heller's psoriasis grew redder. His brow was in a deep, constant crease. Even when he studied *Gemara*, he would pause every few minutes and sigh.

On Thursday night, in the middle of dinner, the phone rang. Shulamis picked up the phone.

"It's for you, *Abba*," she announced.

"Tell whoever it is we are in the middle of dinner," Mrs. Heller said firmly.

"But it's Mr. Robbins, the president," she whispered, her hand over the speaker.

"I'll take it," said Rabbi Heller apologetically. "I won't be able to eat anyway until I speak to him."

He went into the study and closed the door behind him.

"I wonder what the president wants," said Shulamis, picking at her carrots. "I hope it's nothing bad."

"I would like to tell that Mr. Robbins off," said Chaimkel. "*Abba* knows ten times more Torah than Mr. Robbins any day."

"Chaimkel, speak respectfully," Mrs. Heller scolded.

"And I don't like his hair piece either," Chaimkel sneaked in one last word.

"Chaimkel!" his mother shouted at him.

In a few minutes, the study door opened and Rabbi Heller reappeared.

23

"Noach, what's the matter!" gasped his wife.

"*Abba*!" the children screamed and ran to their father.

Rabbi Heller was as white as a ghost. He leaned on his children like an old man and, slightly dazed, sat down at the table. He looked up at his wife.

"They've given me until *Shabbos* to decide," he said. "Either I read from the Knuble *Sefer Torah* on *Shabbos* or I'll be out of a job by Sunday night."

"But they can't do that, can they, *Abba*?" Shulamis asked. "Didn't you sign a paper, a contract?"

"It's their shul," he answered, still looking at his wife. "They say I'm breaking the agreement. Rachel, what shall we do?"

"I'm hungry!" shouted little Baruch, interrupting everything. "I'm starving!"

Rabbi Heller looked down at him and blinked.

"We hardly have anything in the bank," he whispered. "We have no family to help us. What shall I do? What shall I do?"

But Baruch wasn't interested.

"I'm hungry! I'm hungry! Give me cookies! I want cookies!"

Shabbos morning came. The sun shone brilliantly. Rabbi Heller had hardly spoken a word since the call. He was thinking, thinking and worrying. Chaimkel knew his father had hardly slept more than an hour or two since Thursday.

The icicles dripped like little pearls during the January thaw. Rabbi Heller expected to be the first in *shul*.

He opened the door of the sanctuary and paused, astonished. The whole congregation was there! Mr. Robbins sat in the front row, with members of the Board lined up on either side. The second row was the Knuble family. Old Mrs. Knuble and Mrs. Andrea Pfeffer, the president of the sisterhood, were behind the *mechitza*. Meir the Tailor was busy handing out *Siddurim*.

"Good *Shabbos!*" Rabbi Heller greeted the congregation. But he only got a few cool nods and some weak handshakes.

Just Mr. Katz, the *Kohain*, was in a jolly mood.

"Rabbi," he said. "Would you happen to know who's giving the *Kiddush* today?"

Usually, the *Shacharis* service started a half hour late. But that *Shabbos*, with a full house, the service started promptly on time. Mr. Robbins, the president, saw to that.

"It's about time something was done right around here," Mr. Schnitzel muttered to himself.

Rabbi Heller led the service. Chaimkel watched his father. Rabbi Heller's lips moved, his eyes stared at the *Siddur*, but Chaimkel could see that his mind was far, far away.

Disturbing thoughts were indeed tumbling through Rabbi Heller's mind. What would he do if he were sent away from Port Iceberg? He had no other means of earning a living, and he only had enough money to last a few weeks. But then, how could he break Hashem's laws right in front of the Torah in the shul on a

Shabbos? It was unthinkable!

And so it went, back and forth, back and forth, in his mind. Chaimkel saw that his father was sweating heavily. Everyone else saw it, too.

Finally, the time came to take out the *Sefer Torah*. Mr. Goldenberg and Mr. Singer walked up to stand by the *Aron Hakodesh*. Mr. Robbins himself was given the honor of opening the doors.

"*Vayehi bin'soa ha'aron* . . ." the congregation sang lustily.

The walls shook with the voices of the packed congregation. All eyes were on Rabbi Heller.

"*Anna avda d'Kudsha Brich Hu* . . . I am the servant of the Holy Blessed One . . ." intoned Rabbi Heller.

There was utter silence. The congregation waited. Rabbi Heller paused, and gazed at the two *Sifrei Torah*, the brightly crowned *Sefer Torah* of the Knuble family which wasn't kosher, and the small *Sefer Torah* with the frayed mantle that was kosher.

In his mind's eye, he saw the check that came every two weeks for seven hundred and fifty six dollars, after taxes, that kept Baruch in cookies and milk, his wife in dignity, himself in learning.

He reached in . . . and took the small *Sefer Torah*, apologizing under his breath to the Knuble *Sefer Torah*.

The congregation gasped. They all saw what Rabbi Heller had done. He had thrown away a job over two little words that weren't right.

"Rabbi!" yelled Mr. Knuble, the accountant. "Take out the other *Sefer Torah*!"

"Rabbi Heller," Mr. Robbins whispered menacingly under his breath. "Don't cause a fuss. I am ordering you as presiding officer of Anshei Iceberg to take out the Knuble *Sefer Torah*."

Meir the Tailor stepped up to the *bimah*.

"Rabbi, please," he said. "Think of your children."

"I can't," said Rabbi Heller, tears welling up in his eyes. "The law is the law. I can't do what is wrong."

After services, no one stayed for *Kiddush*, not even Mr. Katz. No one shook hands with the rabbi or wished him a good *Shabbos*. He stood forlornly near the *bimah*, surrounded by his children. Only Meir the Tailor came near him. He looked pityingly at the rabbi's family, and shook his head.

"Such nice children," he said and walked away.

Sunday morning, only a few children came to Hebrew School. A secret meeting of the Board was being held in Mr. Goldenberg's house. After school, Rabbi Heller went home and waited.

At exactly one o'clock, the phone rang. Chaimkel watched his father sadly. The ring almost made him jump.

"For you, Noach," said Rachel Heller anxiously. "It's Mr. Robbins."

"I'll take it in the study," said Rabbi Heller.

He closed the door behind him. Mrs. Heller stood nervously near the door. Shulamis and Chaimkel lined up behind her.

"I want cookies!" Baruch yelled from the kitchen.

They could hear Rabbi Heller hang up the phone.

There was a few minutes of silence. Then, the door opened, and Rabbi Heller appeared.

"I am dismissed," he announced. "We have three weeks to move out of the house."

"*Gam zu l'tovah*," said Mrs. Heller. "Everything is for the good. You did what was right."

"Yes," said Rabbi Heller quietly. "I did what was right."

"I want a cookie!" screamed Baruch.

"What shall we do?" said Rabbi Heller. "Where shall we go? How shall we live?"

Without looking at each other, Shulamis and Chaimkel ran to their father and hugged him.

"It will be all right, children," he reassured them, caressing their heads and necks. "I know Hashem will help, but I just don't know how."

Chapter Two

Like a Bolt of Lightning

BECAUSE THERE WAS NO JEWISH day school in Port Iceberg, Shulamis and Chaimkel spent a great deal of time studying with their father privately. He was not just their father but also their teacher and friend.

The Hellers were not a "normal" family. The children did not give their parents problems. There was no nagging, no fights, no spankings. Rabbi and Mrs. Heller had brought up their children to be part of a team, one family. Their life was often hard, and the children knew that everything had to be done together as a family.

On Sunday afternoons, the children spent two hours studying with Rabbi Heller before going off to play with their friends. That afternoon, after lessons, Chaimkel went to his father.

"*Abba*, there is something I need in the *shul*," he said. "Can I borrow the keys?"

Rabbi Heller was deeply involved in studying his *Daf Yomi*. Hardly noticing, he reached into his jacket pocket and gave him the keys without asking why.

"Don't forget to return them," he said.

If he had studied Chaimkel's face, so serious and determined, his curiosity might have been aroused. But Chaimkel quickly grabbed the keys, slipped on his parka and left the house.

Heavy black clouds covered the sky, and the bitter winds made it feel like minus forty degrees. Huge white snow drifts covered the icy streets. Chaimkel slid and slipped and flopped and pushed onward until he reached the *shul*. His face was red and frozen, and his eyebrows were crusted with frost.

He opened the side door of the *shul*. It was warm and dark in the long hallway. Chaimkel lowered his hood and took off his damp gloves. Was what he planned to do right? He carefully washed his hands and entered the *shul*. It was gray and gloomy. The tall windows looked down at him like black, thin shadows.

He quietly walked up to the steps of the *bimah* and stood before the *Aron Hakodesh*. Carefully, he pulled open the blue ark-curtain and slipped open the double doors.

In front of him stood the Knuble *Sefer Torah*. With its tall silver crown, gleaming silver breastplate and pointer, it stood over him like an angel. The velvet mantle was beautifully embroidered in purple and gold, studded with multi-colored glass beads. But Chaimkel did not think of the great silver crown, breastplate or the beautiful mantle. He spoke directly to the *Sefer Torah* rolled up inside.

"Torah, Torah," he spoke softly. "Is it fair? What did my *Abba* do? He wanted to protect your sanctity and honor. He risked his job and our *parnassah* for your sake! Is it fair that he should suffer so much now? Is it right that his eyes should be red from lack of sleep and because he cries when no one is around?

"Torah! You are filled with such holy letters. Each of your words, *Abba* taught me, is filled with Hashem's name. Can't you do something about the situation, Torah? Can't your letters fly up to Heaven and pray for us? How will *Abba* be able to study Torah if he is worried all the time? How can we keep *Shabbos* happily? How will Baruch get cookies?

"Help us, Torah, please! Do something!"

He gently kissed the velvet mantle and closed the ark. He felt strange standing alone in the twilight gloom, as though he were being watched from every side. Quickly, he zippered up his coat and left.

That night, Chaimkel had trouble sleeping. He heard his father pacing nervously in the living room and

snatches of whispered conversation with his mother. The old clock in his room ticked, and each minute meant the time to leave the house was drawing nearer.

Chaimkel tried everything to sleep, counting sheep, making *tzitzis* out of their wool, counting *tzitzis*. But it didn't help.

He closed his eyes and thought of the Knuble *Sefer Torah* open in front of him. The letters were laid out, line after line. How holy each letter was! He understood why his father had sacrificed everything to defend it.

The first word in the Torah was *Beraishis*. He stared at the very first letter, an enormous *bais* as large as an elevator with one glass wall. He entered the elevator, and it gently rocked back and forth and lifted off the ground.

Slowly, it floated upward, through the window, into the bright sunlight and over the rooftop. Gently, it disappeared through the thick wintry clouds over Port Iceberg and then way, way above them, so that their tops looked like strands of cotton in the sunlight. Soon, Port Iceberg was completely out of sight.

Higher and higher rose the *bais* beyond the atmosphere into the black, black expanse of space twinkling with myriad stars and a thick glistening moon. But Chaimkel was not afraid. It was pleasant to be surrounded by the warm, holy letter of the Torah.

Ever higher and higher rose the letter, until there was nothing. No moon, no stars, no light at all. Just Chaimkel, and the vast inky black space stretching forever into the distance.

"What about my *Abba*?" shouted Chaimkel into the great dark expanse.

Then, like a golden flash of lightning, he saw the sky open up with blazing letters.

"Noach ben Chaya Esther l'parnassah tovah!"

Chaimkel smiled and lay back assured. Like a floating balloon losing air, the *bais* started swinging downward, downward, downward, back past the moon and glistening stars, into the atmosphere above the sunlit clouds, through the thick, swirling clouds, down through his bedroom window and back into his warm bed. Chaimkel closed the *bais* and fell into a deep sleep.

The next morning, Chaimkel was awakened by the phone ringing. He looked at the clock. It was six thirty in the morning. Who could be calling at such an early hour? He washed his hands quickly and ran out to answer the phone.

But his father was already there. From his red rimmed eyes, Rabbi Heller looked like he had hardly slept a wink. Chaimkel plopped down on the couch. Rachel Heller drew her robe around her, feeling very worried as she watched her husband.

"Yes, this is Rabbi Heller. Yes, who is this?"

He looked from Chaimkel to his wife. He seemed to have trouble hearing.

"Mr. Simon? Which Mr. Simon? Oh, from Toronto? Sure, I remember you. How are you? Is everything all right? What brings you to call me at this time?"

Rabbi Heller listened intently. Chaimkel couldn't make out the conversation, but it cheered him to see a small smile form on his father's lips.

"Uh, huh. Uh, huh," said Rabbi Heller from time to time. "I understand. Now I understand. You are leaving today. Uh, huh. Yes, why not? Could be. You know, maybe it's a sign from Heaven. Who knows?"

Rabbi Heller's smile deepened, and a rush of color painted his face.

"Yes, I can drive in tomorrow, *bli neder*, to meet your son," he said into the telephone. "But we don't have much money to put down. We're not even sure where we'd live."

He listened for a moment.

"What? Rent your house?" he asked. "For how much?"

His mouth fell open and his eyes widened.

"But that's very reasonable, Mr. Simon," he said. "You're practically giving it away. You don't know what you're doing for us. You are saving our whole family. May Hashem reward you and give you long life. Yes, certainly. Go to *shul*. Be well."

He wrote down a number and put the telephone receiver back very gently.

"You will never believe what happened, Rachel," he said to his wife.

"What? What?" Mrs. Heller and Chaimkel asked in chorus.

"You remember that nice Mr. Simon from that little book store, Sefer-Tov. Well, he decided he wants to

35

retire and move to Eretz Yisrael. But he doesn't want to see Sefer-Tov disappear."

"You mean that little book store around the corner from Bathurst Avenue?" asked Mrs. Heller. "The one that sells kosher *tefillin* and *mezuzos*. And those children's books?"

Yes, that's the one," said Rabbi Heller. "And you know how kind he is to everyone. Well, he wondered who would take it off his hands. Then last night, like a bolt of lightning, he said, he thought of me. He said that with our children to raise, it would be good to live in a *Makom Torah*. Then he asked me when my contract was up."

Rachel Heller and Chaimkel looked at each other stunned. Contract!? They laughed. Contract?

"But it's such a small, out-of-the-way store," Mrs. Heller wondered. "Do you think it will be enough *parnassah*?"

"And do we have any better *parnassah*?" asked Rabbi Heller immediately. "How can we go wrong? Surrounded by holy *sefarim* and *mezuzos*? And he is hardly asking anything for it."

"And we can rent his house?"

"Cheaply."

"And there are proper *yeshivos* and day schools in Toronto for our children, so they can have friends?" asked Mrs. Heller.

"Many friends."

"It is like a hand sent down from Heaven," she said, with wonder in her voice.

"Like a good message that fell from the skies," said Rabbi Heller.

"Like a lightning bolt," whispered Chaimkel. "Just like a bolt of lightning."

Baruch came in, still rubbing his eyes.

"Cookies!!"

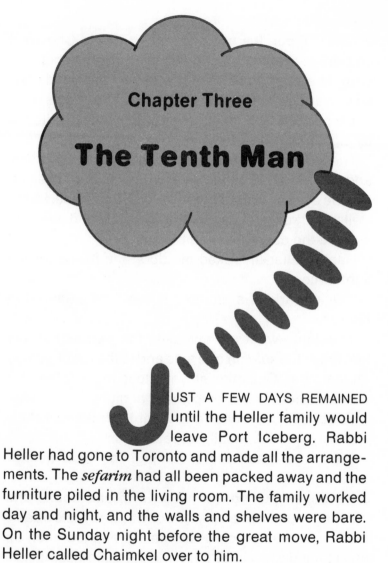

Chapter Three

The Tenth Man

JUST A FEW DAYS REMAINED until the Heller family would leave Port Iceberg. Rabbi Heller had gone to Toronto and made all the arrangements. The *sefarim* had all been packed away and the furniture piled in the living room. The family worked day and night, and the walls and shelves were bare. On the Sunday night before the great move, Rabbi Heller called Chaimkel over to him.

"I have to go down to the *shul* to pick up a few last papers and books," he said. "Please come and help

39

me for a little while."

After supper, the two piled into their old Chevrolet and drove the half mile to Congregation Anshei Iceberg. The skies were leaden, and the fresh wind blew so powerfully that the car shuddered. The streets were snow packed, and on either side, they were walled in by eight foot drifts of snow.

The *shul* was located behind a thin stand of trees, and the darkened windows and gloomy door seemed like the eyes and mouth of some great, sad face. Rabbi Heller parked the car in the *shul* lot, and the two entered the dark, deserted building.

Rabbi Heller unlocked the door and fished for the light switch.

"It's as dark as a haunted house," he muttered to himself.

The lights went on, revealing the narrow hallway that led to the *shul* on one side and to the rabbi's study on the other. Chaimkel stayed close to his father. He was afraid of the big, empty *shul* at night.

Rabbi Heller switched on the lights of his small study and surveyed the small, carpeted room.

"One and a half years," he sighed. "How quickly time flies!"

He began pulling out his *sefarim* and books and packing them into empty cartons. It was a slow task. Each *sefer* was precious to him. He opened each up and studied a few lines here and there. Sometimes, he lingered over a beloved *Tosefos* or a commentary that was especially precious to him. He forgot where he was and who he was. His brow creased, as he lost himself in the Torah.

Chaimkel picked out a *Chumash* and studied the *Rashi*. From time to time, he looked up and watched his father. He knew his father was almost penniless, but how proud he was of him!

My father is an honest man, Chaimkel thought. He is a *Talmid Chacham*, and he is kind to whomever he meets. What more can a son expect from a parent?

Sitting crosslegged on the thick blue carpet, Chaimkel was happy. And in a few days, they would be moving to Toronto!

Finally, Rabbi Heller packed in the last of his books and papers. He glanced at his watch.

"*Oy, gevalt!*" he exclaimed. "It's past eleven o'clock. *Imma* must be worried about us."

Rabbi Heller and Chaimkel quickly donned their heavy coats and hats, closed the lights and headed for the exit. Even with the dim lights on, the hallway was shadowy. They rushed to leave the building.

Rabbi Heller closed the hall light, pitching them into deep blackness. He pushed open the outside door.

"What is this?" he muttered.

No matter how hard he pushed, even with Chaimkel's help, the door remained stuck, as though a great hand was holding them in. Finally, they managed to open it just a fraction of an inch. Rabbi Heller peered through the crack.

"I can't believe it!" he exclaimed.

"What is it?" asked Chaimkel, peering through the

crack in the door.

During the three hours they had been there, a quiet, steady snow had fallen. And fallen. And fallen. And it was still falling. The snow was more than a foot high, blocking the door and stranding their old Chevrolet in the lot.

"There's no way we can open the door now," said Rabbi Heller. "And even if we do, how will we get home?"

"What shall we do?" asked Chaimkel nervously.

"There's no choice," said Rabbi Heller, flicking the hall lights back on. "We must stay here tonight."

The lower level of Congregation Anshei Iceberg contained a long, narrow social hall, a small kitchen, a storage room and wash rooms.

Rabbi Heller switched on the lights and surveyed the scene. Bare tables and chairs were scattered around. A broken piano stood half open in the corner.

"Where will we sleep?" asked Chaimkel.

"We'll have to make do," his father answered.

Chaimkel and Rabbi Heller piled together as many old coats and jackets as they could find. It looked like all the leftovers from Anshei Iceberg's sixty years of rummage sales were piled in the storage rooms.

"We'll sleep like in the old days," said Rabbi Heller and laughed.

"Old days?" asked Chaimkel.

"Yes. When scholars studied in the *Bais Medrash*, they covered themselves with coats, put towels under their heads for pillows and slept on benches."

42

"Didn't they have bedrooms?" asked Chaimkel, imagining sleeping on the hard benches upstairs.

His father, meanwhile, was making a temporary bed by lining up two rows of four chairs. He laid tablecloths for sheets, and more tablecloths for pillows.

"Some did and some didn't," said Rabbi Heller. "But they didn't want to waste time that could be used to study Torah. They would spend the whole week studying, eating and sleeping in the *Bais Medrash*, just not to waste an extra precious moment of Torah."

"Wow!" exclaimed Chaimkel. "Is that how they learn Torah in Toronto?"

Rabbi Heller grunted without answering.

The "beds" were ready. Rabbi Heller set them next to each other. He was so tired from teaching, packing books and making calls, he could hardly keep his eyes open.

"I could lie on the bare floor and fall asleep," he told Chaimkel wearily.

Chaimkel's father went to the switch box and closed all the lights. It was pitch black.

"No, no!" protested Chaimkel. "Please leave one light on. I'm afraid."

Rabbi Heller sighed. He got up and turned on a light near the exit, throwing a dim glow over the room. He smiled reassuringly.

"What is there to be afraid of?" he asked. "Upstairs is a *shul* with an *Aron Hakodesh*. Where would Hashem watch over you better than here?"

Chaimkel and his father climbed into their makeshift

beds and covered themselves. Rabbi Heller said the bedtime *berachah* of *Hamapil*, turned over and in a few minutes was snoring peacefully. Chaimkel leaned on his elbow and watched his father whom he loved very much. He even liked to watch his father sleep, because he knew that when a good person sleeps it is also a *mitzvah*.

But Chaimkel himself couldn't sleep. The chairs were too hard, and with his father's snoring, he felt suddenly very alone. The large, dim, silent underground room was spooky. He closed his eyes for a second, but they popped open. He imagined something was crawling up to him from the shadows.

He thought about the *shul* just upstairs, the *shul* he knew so well. He could trace every inch, the steps before the *Aron Hakodesh*, the tall, gray windows, the *Yahrzeit* tablet, the mural in the hallway.

What was that!?

He jumped awake. It sounded like . . . someone walking upstairs. He listened hard.

Silence.

His imagination must be at work. It was probably just the snow settling on the roof.

He looked at his father for reassurance. Poor *Abba*! He had so much on his mind. Even when he snored, he frowned and his brow creased. Chaimkel wondered what his father was dreaming about.

Meanwhile, Chaimkel couldn't sleep a wink. His eyes wandered over the gloomy basement, and he turned over, closing his eyes momentarily. He thought about the old days in Europe, and the hard benches they slept on. The benches at Anshei Iceberg were all padded with purple cushions.

His eyes popped open!

There were definitely footsteps upstairs! He could hear someone talking . . . a few people . . . someone walking. Burglars! Maybe they would open the *Aron Hakodesh*.

Chaimkel turned to his father to wake him. His father had stopped snoring. His face was relaxed, and Chaimkel knew he was in a deep, peaceful slumber. The footsteps upstairs had stopped.

Absolute quiet.

How could he wake his tired father for such . . . nonsense? It was surely nothing, just the old building creaking. One of the men had once told him that even after many years the building still shifted and creaked, beams sagged and groaned. The footsteps were his imagination. His father hadn't slept this well in days. How could he wake him up?

Chaimkel raised his head again and surveyed the room. It looked so dark and sad now. The building had been built almost sixty years before. The walls were painted bright yellow and white. How many weddings had taken place here? How many *Bar Mitzvahs*? How many *Kiddushes*? He began multiplying sixty years times the weeks in a year.

Hmmphh, he thought to himself. Other boys count sheep, but I count *Kiddushes*. Why can't I sleep?

What was that!?

45

He could hear the sound of talking upstairs in the *shul*! There was no mistaking the voices. Buildings creaked, but they didn't talk! A chill raced down his spine, and he jumped up like a bolt.

"*Abba*! *Abba*!" he whispered loudly, without thinking. "There's someone upstairs. Quick!"

"Harrumph, grrummble, harrumph," said his father. "Give me another ten minutes. Please. Harrumph." Then his father drew a sweater over his head and turned his back to Chaimkel.

Chaimkel didn't know what to do. He was frightened to death. But how could he wake up his father? Hadn't someone given up a fortune not to wake his father? His poor father was so, so tired. How could he do this to him?

Chaimkel listened closely. Was it his imagination again? No, he could hear voices clearly. More than one, or even two. Who could it be? He thought he knew. One of the motorcycle gangs that always roared down King Street must have decided to visit the *shul* on a lark; he knew they did such things.

He thought immediately of the *Sifrei Torah*. At a fire, people risked their lives for the *Sifrei Torah*. Wasn't this just like a fire? Who knows what damage these gangs could do? Chaimkel made up his mind. Motorcycle gang or not, he must run upstairs and throw himself in front of the *Aron Hakodesh* to protect the *Sifrei Torah*.

In his stocking feet, he padded silently through the dim social hall, through the black hallway and up the carpeted stairs to the *shul*. It was eerie; the voices were louder now. He inched to the entrance of the *shul*, opened the door slightly and peered in.

What he saw made his hair stand on end.

There was just enough light from the *Ner Tamid* lamp and *Yahrzeit* bulbs to make out the people in the room. One, two, three, four, five, six, seven, eight, nine. Yes, nine old men sat scattered among the benches. Some held *Siddurim* in their hands. Chaimkel did not recognize them. They all looked deathly pale.

Chaimkel peered through the slightly opened door and listened.

"Say, Harry, what time is the *minyan* supposed to start?"

Harry stared at his watch and shook his head.

"Wait, wait, wait. Always wait."

"Boy, that was some fireworks at Pearl Harbor," said another old man. "Didn't the Americans think the Japanese would really attack?"

"Do you think Diefenbaker will call new elections?" piped up another.

"I never did like that Herbert Hoover," grumbled another man in a brown felt hat. "I'm glad they put Roosevelt in."

"Who's giving *Kiddush* this week?" asked yet another white haired man.

Pearl Harbor? Diefenbaker? Herbert Hoover? What were they talking about? wondered Chaimkel to himself.

And then it struck him who they were. Like icicles racing up his spine, he froze in fright and turned to run back down to his father. But in his panic, his elbow banged loudly against the wooden *shul* door.

Crack!

The sound shot across the empty *shul* like a crack of lightning. All the old men turned to the door and stared at Chaimkel with their big, white eyes. He wanted to run, but their ghostly, pale faces held him.

"Why, there's a youngster," said Harry. "Come in, *yingelle*, come in."

Chaimkel wanted to hide, run, get away from those white faces. But they stared so deeply at him, he couldn't run. Shakily, Chaimkel slipped into the *shul* and stood near the door.

"Don't be afraid of us, young man. We won't hurt you," said the man with white hair, who looked a lot like Meir the Tailor. "Have a seat. Join us awhile."

The other ghostly men nodded. They seemed so kindly that Chaimkel felt calmer. He sat down on the edge of a bench, ready to leap up.

"Wh-who are you?" he asked one of the men, who except for his whiteness looked like any old man in a *shul*.

"You've never seen us before?" he asked.

"Never."

"He's the new rabbi's son, the one they fired," another old man called out. "What does he know about us? There are so many rabbis coming and going, they never hear us. Or about us."

"Who are you?" Chaimkel pleaded. "Please tell me."

"We are the old *shul* members of Congregation

Anshei Iceberg," the old man began.

"You mean you are still members?" asked Chaimkel.

"No," he chortled. "We were members before you were born. Even before your Poppa was born. We were here many, many years ago."

"How long ago?" asked Chaimkel, forgetting his fear.

"Oh, some of us twenty years, others thirty. Max there was a founding member. And then all of us passed on from this freezing world."

They all nodded their heads, confirming Chaimkel's worst fears.

"Then what are you doing here?" asked Chaimkel, trembling.

All the men stared at Chaimkel sadly, as though they were ashamed to speak. They did not scare Chaimkel. They seemed so . . . helpless.

"Please tell me," pleaded Chaimkel.

The man in the felt hat looked up from his book. He peered over his reading glasses.

"We all used to attend services for many, many years, for which they gave us much credit in Heaven," he said.

"So what are you still doing in Port Iceberg?" asked Chaimkel. "Why aren't you in Gan Eden?"

"We were all judged by the Holy Court," explained Max, with a sad, kindly smile. "They decided that because of one sin we did repeatedly we must return to the *shul*."

"What sin?"

49

"We always gathered early on *Shabbos* morning and waited for a *minyan*. The rabbi used to sit up at the *bimah*, like your father does, and study the *Parshah*. Shy of us, I think. Well, each *Shabbos* morning we would spend a half hour, maybe even an hour, waiting."

"Waiting?"

"For a *minyan*. But instead of opening a book to study some Torah or a little *Nashi*—"

"*Nashi*? *Nashi*? What's *Nashi*?" wondered Chaimkel. "You mean *Rashi*?"

"Whatever," the man continued. "But instead of using the time to study, we just sat around and told stories. You know, shot the breeze."

"Shot the breeze?" asked Chaimkel. "On *Shabbos*? With a gun?"

"No, not with a gun. Just talk. About politics, town gossip, business, world events, whatever came to mind. I remember one fellow who used to tell stories about the Russo-Japanese War. Good stories, those. Well, we wasted years and years, just running at the mouth, killing time."

Chaimkel nodded sympathetically, remembering all the games he'd played with Shulamis and Baruch before *davening* in the classrooms.

"I'll tell you why we're here," shouted a tall, thin man and jumped up, but immediately, he grabbed for his leg and sat down heavily. "Darn leg. The cold always does this." He looked up at Chaimkel. "We're here, because our punishment is to wait forever for a *minyan*."

50

"Yes," agreed Max with a sigh. "Each night, we appear in the *shul*, just nine of us. And we have to wait and wait and wait for a *minyan*."

"And what's worse," grumbled the tall man, "we have to tell each other stories and gossip the whole time. Every night, we hear the same story about how Max got shot through the hat during the First World War."

The men all groaned.

"And if I have to hear about Oscar's gall bladder operation again I'll just scream," said Max.

"What are you complaining about?" answered Oscar sharply. "Do I always have to hear about how many sets of Scandinavian furniture you sold last week. Every night, the same breakfront. Every night —phooey!"

"And the Herbert Hoover stories—" spoke up another.

"And the town council politics."

"And those stories about Rebbetzin Scheiner—"

The men started arguing among themselves. Chaimkel watched them. They seemed to forget completely about him. They bickered, called each other names, switched seats. They seemed so high-strung, nervous and sad that Chaimkel felt pity for them.

"Wait!" Chaimkel suddenly shouted. His voice rang out strong and clear, in sharp contrast to their pale, weak voices. "Has anyone ever met you before like I did? Did anyone ever see you?"

The men all looked at him with gloomy, white eyes.

"No, never," said Max. "You are the first."

An idea flashed through Chaimkel's mind.

"Then it is no accident," he said. "You're waiting for a *minyan*. No one ever slept here at Anshei Iceberg for the night. My father is downstairs sleeping. If he came up here and joined you, wouldn't that make a *minyan*?"

"Yes! Yes!" the men cried excitedly.

"Then, if he came up and joined you, you could finally escape from Anshei Iceberg and go to Heaven?" asked Chaimkel.

"Oh, yes, yes," they answered, almost crying. "Oh, yes, finally. Please call him!"

Suddenly, he remembered to whom he was talking— spirits!

"May I leave you?" he asked, his voice becoming timid. "I mean, to g-go downstairs and call him?"

They stared at him, and then shouted, "Yes! Go, Chaimkel, go! Go!"

Chaimkel did not wait an extra second. He shot up from the bench, ran through the doors, through the blackened hallways and down the stairs to the lower level. His father would have to forgive him for what he was about to do.

He ran to his snoring father.

"*Abba*!" he shouted. "*Abba*, wake up! Please!"

"Huh! What is it!?" Rabbi Heller's eyes opened, and he came awake. "Chaimkel! What's the matter? What time is it?"

"*Abba, Abba*," Chaimkel said breathlessly. "I must show you something. Come upstairs with me. I have to

52

show you something. Please come right away."

"Show me something? Upstairs?" asked Rabbi Heller, uncomprehending. "What's upstairs at this time of night?"

Chaimkel was afraid to tell his father. He knew what he would say.

"Come, *Abba*!" he just pleaded. "Please come with me quickly. It's so important!"

Rabbi Heller stared at his frantic son for a moment, then he washed his hands and followed Chaimkel up the stairs.

"A *minyan*, a *minyan*," thought Chaimkel to himself. "My *Abba* will make a *minyan*, and let the *neshamos* fly up to Gan Eden."

They rushed down the hallway and stood before the doors of the *shul*. Rabbi Heller swung the door open and peered in.

"What is it?" he asked impatiently. "What is it you want me to see?"

Chaimkel squeezed under his father's arm and looked in. Where were his friends!? There was not a soul there, just row after row of empty benches.

Rabbi Heller gave Chaimkel a queer look.

"What is this all about, Chaimkel?" he wanted to know. "Why did you wake me in middle of the night?"

Chaimkel didn't know what to say. The *neshamos* were gone! They had probably disappeared the moment his father had opened the door.

"I-I thought I saw, I mean, heard something," he stammered.

54

"Heard? Heard what?"

"F-footsteps. I heard someone talk, I mean, walk..."
He felt foolish.

Rabbi Heller looked down at his son, ran his hand over his *yarmulke* and curly hair, and laughed.

"Oh, Chaimkel, you dreamer," he said with a gentle smile on his face. "You must have been imagining again! Walking? Talking? The snow, Chaimkel. That's all it was, the snow. And the building groaning."

Chaimkel gave one last look into the *shul* he would never see again.

"Yes," agreed Chaimkel. "It must have just been the *shul* groaning."

He followed his father back down the steps, stopping just once to rub his sore elbow.

"*Abba*, who is Diefenbaker?" he asked.

Chapter Four

A Late Customer

SEFER TOV JEWISH BOOKSTORE was on a side street in Toronto, Canada, and not a very busy one at that. In fact, many people passed the store for years without even knowing it was there. It was a small store, with a few *mezuzos, tefillin, Siddurim, Chumashim* and *Gemaras*, some carefully chosen children's books, some *Kiddush* cups, candlesticks and many, many *sefarim*.

Rabbi Heller barely eked out a living from the store. Each night, he would count what he had sold and how much money he had. It was very little, too little most of the time. Besides, many people took on credit and then took a long time to pay.

Chaimkel loved the store. He knew every corner, closet and hiding place. He knew which mice lived where. He knew where the old greeting cards were and where to find the collection of *posul mezuzos* that had been set aside.

After school, he went straight to the store to help straighten up. His father had set up a *shtender* in the corner of the store, and when no customers appeared, he would sit and study his *Daf Yomi* or review the *Parshah*. When he concentrated, he wrapped himself over the *shtender* like a skinny blanket.

Rabbi Heller was very worried. Running a book store was much harder than he had expected. Bills mounted. Chaimkel heard his parents talking about how the suppliers in New York were going to stop sending books. Chaimkel watched his father closely. He saw his sideburns turning gray and his wrinkles growing deeper. In January, when the snows fell and people stayed home, his father would look into the empty cash box at night and sigh.

One day after school, Chaimkel came into the store and found it empty. Had *Abba* left early and forgotten to lock up?

The lights were still on. Chaimkel was about to shut them off when he heard a voice, his father's voice, coming from the back room. He was talking to some- one. Chaimkel approached silently.

"*Ribono Shel Olam*," his father was pleading. "You know I could have tried to get a position in another small town, but I didn't. I agreed to struggle with a tiny bookstore so we could stay in a *Makom Torah*, raise our children with *Yiras Shamayim* and make proper *shidduchim*.

"But do you call this business? I strive so hard to have proper *sefarim* that teach Your sacred Word, but what good does that do me when my suppliers call for money and my pockets are empty? I had one customer today. One! In a whole day! One *yarmulke* sold for three dollars. One dollar profit! How can I feed my wife and children on one dollar a day? It is Your *Chumashim* and *tefillin* I sell. Won't You help me?"

Tears welled in Chaimkel's eyes. He wanted to open the door, run to his *Abba*, hug him and tell him how much he loved him. But he did not dare show he had heard anything. Quietly, he slipped back outside, waited a few minutes on Bathurst Street and then reentered the store. Rabbi Heller was back at his *shtender*. He saw Chaimkel and smiled. But he could not hide the redness around his eyes.

One afternoon in late March, Rabbi Heller took Chaimkel aside after school.

"I have to leave early tonight," he said. "Please watch the store for me."

Chaimkel hesitated.

"But I don't know how," he said.

Rabbi Heller laughed sadly.

"I just hope you have someone to take care of," he

said. "Here, I'll show you."

He taught Chaimkel how to mark up a sale and how to use the calculator to figure the taxes. He showed him the different types of *mezuzos* and how to carefully roll, not fold, them.

"But what if I make a mistake?" asked Chaimkel. "Maybe I'll make you lose money."

"Let there just be customers," prayed Rabbi Heller.

It was past four thirty, and the store closed at six. In his heart, Chaimkel hoped no customers would come. And no one did.

"Oh, I'm wishing away our *parnassah*!" thought Chaimkel. "No, no, Hashem. Send someone. Anyone!"

Fifteen minutes before closing time, an elderly gentleman wearing a handkerchief in his lapel and a snow white mustache entered the store.

"Can I help you?" asked Chaimkel timidly.

The man gave Chaimkel an impatient glance.

"No, young man, I am just browsing," he said, the tone of his voice showing he didn't want to be bothered.

Chaimkel hid his nose in the pages of the book he was reading, watching the man through the corner of his eye.

Buy something, he sent thought messages to the man. Anything!

There was silence in the store. The clock ticked toward closing time. And then, the man gave out a shout.

"I found it! I found it!" he yelled excitedly.

Chaimkel jumped up, startled. The man was crouched behind one of the book islands, peering at some books. Chaimkel moved closer to see what was so exciting. He was stopped by a strange sight. The man was completely bent over, a large magnifying glass in his hand, and studying the small letters in a *sefer*. He was concentrating so hard he didn't even notice Chaimkel.

Chaimkel returned to the counter, hoping. In a few minutes, the man came over to the counter, waving the *sefer* in the air.

"I've been looking for this *sefer* for years," he said. "Everywhere! Yerushalayim, Bnai Brak, Boro Park. And I finally found it. Here!"

Chaimkel was so excited he could hardly contain himself.

"*Baruch Hashem*," he whispered under his breath. "A customer."

"How much is it, young man?" he asked.

Chaimkel noticed that he spoke with a refined tone. Chaimkel opened to the front inside cover where Rabbi Heller usually pencilled in the prices. There was nothing written.

Nervously, Chaimkel looked inside the back cover, then he leafed through the front pages. There wasn't a price to be found. The man was growing impatient.

"I-I don't know," stammered Chaimkel, feeling stupid. "There is usually a price, but I don't see one. Oh—" His mouth fell open in dismay.

"What's the matter?" demanded the man, dangling

the magnifying glass in front of him.

Chaimkel's face fell.

"This is the third volume of a set," he said. "I can't sell it separately."

"But I have the rest of the set," insisted the man. "It is the third volume that I've been missing for years, and here it is!"

"But—"

"No buts! This is the volume I need, and this is what I will take. Are you worried for the set? Why worry? Here, I'll pay for the whole set."

He took out a flaming red Canadian fifty dollar bill.

"Take the money!"

Fifty dollars! Chaimkel could hardly speak. He remembered now that the whole set was just thirty-two dollars.

"It is only thirty-two dollars for the whole set," he blurted. "I must get you change."

Chaimkel ran back to the office where the money box was hidden in a bottom drawer. He opened it up. There was a five dollar bill, four singles and a few dollars in change. The whole day's sales. Even with all that he was still short fifty cents for change. He dug into his own pocket and found a quarter, plus a stamp worth thirty cents. He rushed back out.

The man was gone!

He hadn't even waited for his change or the rest of the set. Fifty dollars for one book! It was too much money for one book.

He raced out into the street. A light, soft snow was

falling, twinkling in the street lights.

He ran to Bathurst Street.

There was the man, waiting at a bus stop. He was still bent over, peering at the *sefer*. The thick magnifying glass was held in the other hand. Chaimkel ran towards him.

"Sir, you forgot your change," said Chaimkel breathlessly. "There are eighteen dollars coming to you."

Chaimkel looked closely at the man and caught his breath, jumping back in fright.

The man looked so different. His handkerchief was gone, his mustache was pale and his brows curled over his eyes. And he looked so much older than he had just minutes before.

"Change? Change?" the old shrunken man answered sharply. "I don't get any change. That is store business. This isn't the store. Keep it. Tell your father to keep it! Don't bother. Don't bother!"

Chaimkel stepped back. He was frightened of this strange man.

Suddenly, the bus slid up silently to the bus stop like a great boat. The old man jumped in, and the bus departed.

Rabbi Heller returned to the store a few minutes after six.

"Any business?" he asked.

Chaimkel took out the fifty dollars and showed it to his father. He told him the whole story.

Rabbi Heller could hardly believe his ears. Fifty dollars! When had he ever seen fifty dollars at Sefer-Tov?

He made Chaimkel tell him the story over and over again.

Chaimkel never saw the man again, but he often thought about him. Who was he? Could it have been Eliyahu Hanavi? asked Shulamis.

No one knew. But the Heller family celebrated a truly happy *Shabbos* that week.

Chapter Five

Shaymess Mountain

BUSINESS WAS AT A STANDSTILL
at Sefer-Tov. It was after *Shavuos*, and many people had
left for their cottages. No schools bought books; no
people moved into houses in need of *mezuzos*; no one
needed gifts for *Bar Mitzvahs*. Books came in, bills
came in, the rent was due. But no customers.

Chaimkel watched his father pace back and forth in
the empty store, straightening here, tidying there. But
for whom?

Sundays were usually busy, but now it was *sha-shtill*

quiet. On Monday, only two people came into the store. Tuesday and Wednesday? No one! Rabbi Heller shuffled through the bills, reviewed the *Parshah*—and worried.

Chaimkel thought and thought. What could he do to help?

Then he got his bright idea.

"*Abba*," Chaimkel began cautiously as his father looked up from his *Chumash*. "I have an idea."

"An idea?" Rabbi Heller sniffed suspiciously. "What kind of idea?"

"I was thinking," said Chaimkel. "There are other book stores in Toronto. But do any of them deal in used *sefarim*?"

"Used *sefarim*? Old books?"

"Sure, why not!" answered Chaimkel with excitement. "There must be hundreds of Jews in Toronto with *sefarim* they don't want or need. We could buy them for just a little money, and then sell them for a profit. Why, it would hardly cost us anything!"

"Hmmm." Rabbi Heller stroked his beard. "I don't know."

Chaimkel was excited now.

"And we would be the only book store in Toronto to deal in used *sefarim*," he continued. "People would come from all over. Why, we could make a living just from the *sefarim*."

"But—"

"What can we lose?" Chaimkel insisted. "Shulamis and I will make a few posters and put them up in the butcher shop and bakery asking for used *sefarim*. In no time at all, we'll have a large selection."

"Well," said Rabbi Heller doubtfully, still stroking his beard. "I don't see what harm it can do. Business can't get much worse than it is now."

"And *Abba*, one more thing," said Chaimkel and paused.

"Out with it, Chaimkel!" said Rabbi Heller. "What do you want to ask?"

"Well," said Chaimkel. "Since it was my idea, and Shulamis and I will be doing the work, could we possibly call it Chaimkel and Shulamis Heller's Used *Sefer* Division of Sefer-Tov, Ltd.?"

Rabbi Heller nodded with an amused smile.

"Why not?" he said, with a shrug of his shoulders. "Maybe a name change will bring new luck to Sefer-Tov!"

Chaimkel and Shulamis did not waste time. Right that afternoon they began painting yellow posters with heavy black letters:

CHAIMKEL AND SHULAMIS HELLER'S
USED SEFARIM AND BOOKS!
(A new division of Sefer-Tov Ltd.)
BRING IN YOUR OLD SEFARIM FOR CASH
(Not too much cash, though)
WE BUY USED SEFARIM CHEAPLY!!!
(We are the only Jewish book store
in Toronto to provide this service!)

Shulamis, who was artistic, made an appropriate design for each poster. Mrs. Heller looked over each poster and made suggestions. Even Rabbi Heller had to smile. In a few days, even before *Shabbos*, more than twenty posters were put up. Chaimkel couldn't wait to see what the results would be.

Sunday morning, Chaimkel drove with his father to the store. It was a warm, golden summer day. Rabbi Heller stopped his car suddenly in front of the store entrance.

"What are all those cartons doing in front of the store!?" he exclaimed.

Chaimkel didn't even wait for his father to park. He jumped out of the stopped car and ran to the boxes. There was a note on top. "For Sefer-Tov," it read. "Free of charge."

He ran back to his father. He was so excited he could hardly speak.

"Used *sefarim, Abba*!" he burst out. "And they don't even want money!"

"Really!" answered Rabbi Heller, locking his car door and hurrying to the store. "That's wonderful. I can't believe it!"

Hurriedly, Chaimkel and his father carted the four heavy cartons into the crowded little store.

"Whew!" whistled Chaimkel, letting one down none too gently. "These weigh a ton."

Excitedly, they opened the first carton. Rabbi Heller peered in and jumped back in dismay.

"Oh, no!" he exclaimed. The carton was filled with

old, shredding *Chumashim* and *Siddurim*, yellowed crumbling pages from *Tehillim*, ripped off *tzitzis* and corners of *talleisim*. Dust rose from the box like a little golden cloud, stuffing their noses.

"Who will ever buy this?" cried Rabbi Heller. "This is *shaymess!*"

"Maybe the other cartons are better," said Chaimkel hopefully, quickly opening them. But it was all the same. Piles of worn *tefillin* straps, pages from *Siddurim*, ripped covers from *Gemaras*.

"What will we do with this?" asked Rabbi Heller. "Our store is so overcrowded already, and this will just take up space."

Chaimkel was filled with dread. What had he gotten his father into?

"Maybe we can return it," he said. "Let's see if there's an address attached."

They checked through the boxes, pressing their hands along the inside edges of the cartons. Chaimkel found a closed envelope and pulled it out expectantly.

"Look, they've left a note," he cried.

"Open it quick," said his father.

Chaimkel ripped open the envelope and opened the note. In bold letters were two words. "*Yasher koach.*"

"*Yasher koach!*" screamed Rabbi Heller, "*Yasher koach*!? What am I going to do with all this *shaymess*?"

Before Chaimkel could answer, there was a thump at the door, followed by another.

"What was that?" Rabbi Heller asked.

Chaimkel raced to the door just in time to see a car

speeding away. Chaimkel tried to run after it, but it was too fast. With dread, Chaimkel opened up the new boxes.

More *shaymess*!

"Everyone's dropping off their *shaymess* here!" he groaned.

The phone didn't stop ringing the whole day at Sefer-Tov.

"Do you take *shaymess*?"

"Can you get rid of an old *tallis* for me?"

"What do I do with these old books my *bubba's bubba* left me?"

All through the day, cars stopped and dropped off boxes of *shaymess* right on the sidewalk.

"Stop! Stop!" screamed Rabbi Heller, panicking. "What am I going to do with all these *shaymess*?"

That night, Rabbi Heller was very edgy. Not only did Sefer-Tov have almost no business, it was now crowded with fifteen boxes of other people's *shaymess*. And there was not even one salable *sefer*!

His father looked at him sternly.

"This you call a business?" he said. "This is a headache!"

"Where does *shaymess* go?" asked Chaimkel.

"It's supposed to be buried in a Jewish cemetery, with great respect," his father answered. "We can't just throw it out. How will I ever find place for all of it?"

When Shulamis heard what had happened, she resigned.

"It was your dumb idea," she insisted. "I just handled

the advertising, nothing else."

Chaimkel felt like crawling into a hole. He was all alone.

So now it was his business. Some business!

The next morning, right after *davening*, Chaimkel rushed down to the store. He took one look and groaned.

Piled up in front of Sefer-Tov were another six cartons. Chaimkel did not wait to bring them into the store. Right on the street he opened a few and peered in. *Shaymess*! *Shaymess, shaymess, shaymess*! Kilos and kilos of it, ripped, browned, crumbling, unusable.

Rabbi Heller came running.

"More *shaymess*!? More!?" he wailed. "What am I going to do with it? I can't even bring it into the store. There is no room left in the basement. What have you done to me, Chaimkel?"

But what could Rabbi Heller do? Dump the boxes on the street? With so many pages of Hashem's Name and sacred *pesukim*? No, never! He was stuck with them.

"We must get rid of the *shaymess*," Rabbi Heller muttered as he unlocked the front door. "Chaimkel, you look out for customers, we should only be so lucky, while I get on the phone and try to get some help."

Rabbi Heller slipped off his jacket, sat down in the frayed blue desk chair in the back office and picked up the phone. The door was open, and Chaimkel could hear everything.

"Hello, hello," Rabbi Heller was saying. "Is the rabbi there? Hello? Hello?"

There was a momentary pause while the rabbi was called to the phone. Rabbi Heller explained the problem. Then, there were a few moments of silence.

"Yes, I understand," Rabbi Heller finally said. "The Board wouldn't . . . Whom should I ask? The *chazan*? Well, if you think so. It's his department, I see. Yes, thank you."

Rabbi Heller started dialing again.

"Hello, is Cantor Chirenboim there?" he asked. "An answering service? I don't want an answering service, I want the *chazan*. It's urgent. Where did he go? The health club! At this time of the morning. All right, let me have the number, please."

Rabbi Heller dialed for the third time.

"Hello! Hello! Could you get me Cantor Chirenboim. You have to page him? He's on the jogging track? Yes, yes. I'll wait."

There was a long pause. Just at that moment, a man with dark glasses and a straw hat ran up to the door, dropped a carton and ran off.

"Wait! Wait!" yelled Chaimkel, racing out to catch him. "No more *shaymess*! Please, no more *shaymess*!"

But it was too late. The motor of the getaway car was running, and the man jumped in and raced off. Sadly, Chaimkel slunk back into the store. His father was still waiting.

"Hello, Cantor Chirenboim," he said at last. "How are you, Reb Dovid? This is Noach Heller. I have a problem. What? You want to know how I like your new *niggun*? Wait—"

But it was too late. Chaimkel knew Cantor Chirenboim. Whoever met him had to hear his latest *niggun*.

"Yes, yes, that's a nice boim, boim, boim," said Rabbi Heller. "A little heavy on the diddle, diddle, dee, but the bum dee dum is fine. Listen, Reb Dovid, I have a great problem. I need your help!"

Chaimkel's back was to the door, so he heard, not saw, when another thud hit. He didn't want to look.

Quickly, Rabbi Heller explained how *shaymess* was piling up.

"What? Speak to the *shammas*?" a troubled Rabbi Heller was saying. "But the rabbi said . . . Yes, I know you're not the *shammas*. A great *chazan*. Yes, I know. Please don't be insulted. Yes, give me his number please."

Again the phone was dialed. Poor *Abba*!

"Hello, *shammas*?" said Rabbi Heller. "Help! I have *shaymess* piling up like a mountain! What? Why am I calling you? Who else should I call? You have too much *shaymess* already? But what shall I do? The whole city is dropping its *shaymess* here. Yes, I know it has to be buried. The *gabbai* in charge? Yes, please! Give me his number."

Poor *Abba*! thought Chaimkel. What a mess I've gotten him into. The phone was dialed again. Chaimkel knew his father got very nervous when he spoke to a *gabbai*, any *gabbai*, ever since he had been rabbi in Port Iceberg. This time, Rabbi Heller closed the door so Chaimkel couldn't hear.

"Please, *Ribono Shel Olam*," prayed Chaimkel. "Get us out of this mess!"

In a few minutes, Rabbi Heller opened the door and stalked out. He walked right past Chaimkel and stood at the open door. Chaimkel approached him.

"What happened, *Abba*?" he asked.

"Mr. Greenland said they could open a special place for our *shaymess*, but it would cost five hundred dollars."

"Five hundred dollars!!!"

"That's right," sighed Rabbi Heller, on the verge of tears. "We are barely managing to pay rent, food and tuition. And now, plunk! Five hundred dollars."

Chaimkel gulped and looked at the front sidewalk of the store. There were five more cartons waiting for them.

That night, Chaimkel tossed and turned in his bed. Rabbi Heller was not home. He had told his wife he was going to wait up all night in front of the store to stop other people from leaving their cartons of *shaymess*. He hadn't yelled at Chaimkel, but every so often their eyes met for an instant, and the thoughts traveled silently.

Poor *sefarim*! thought Chaimkel. Once they had been so proud and used. The holiest prayers started their long ride to Hashem's throne from their pages. They had been kissed, gold-stamped, cherished. Now, they were browned and crumbling.

The whole day Chaimkel had searched among the

sefarim, trying to find at least a few he could sell. Now, lying in his bed, he thought about a *sefer* he had found, an old, large *Tanach* with a Yiddish translation inside. It was a huge *sefer*, more than fifty years old, with brown covers like doors. Chaimkel opened the great *Yehoshua* door and entered.

Oh, no! There was Sefer-Tov, but his father was nowhere in sight. Boxes and boxes of *shaymess* were piled against the sides of Sefer-Tov, almost higher than a man. Hundreds of people from all over Toronto were heading for the store, men, women, and children carrying more *shaymess*.

"Stop! Stop!" yelled Chaimkel. "There's no room!"

But the people kept on bringing boxes.

"This is the first place that was ever interested in *shaymess*," one man called out to the frantic Chaimkel. "There are tons of *shaymess* in Toronto, and no one wants it. Except Sefer-Tov. Think of the *mitzvah!*"

"But—"

It was too late. The boxes kept piling up, higher and higher. People were bringing ladders and piling boxes on the roof; it was almost impossible to tell that a store was there.

There was a traffic jam on the corner of Bathurst and Woburn as more cars came. Everyone had a *sefer*, a *Chumash*, a *Siddur*.

People were singing to each other:

Bring the boxes!
Bring the books!

Bring the *sefarim*
from all the nooks!

Where were all these *sefarim* coming from? wondered Chaimkel. He stopped several boxes of *sefarim*.

"Who are you?" he asked.

"We are seven *Machzorim* from Bloor Street," answered one carton.

"Fifteen *Siddurim* from the old Nerayever *shul*!" cried another.

"*Posul tefillin* from Downsview!" yelled another.

A huge carton came swinging by.

"Who are you?" asked Chaimkel.

"Lubavitch sent us," it answered quickly.

"Used J.E.P. guides here," piped up another.

"Zay sent us from zee Montreal," said a box marked with French words.

Chaimkel looked up. Aaggh!! The boxes were piling higher and higher, sky high! They must be six stories high now, and growing taller by the minute. Huge ladders were lifted as people climbed higher and higher to pile up their *shaymess*.

"When will it ever stop?" wondered Chaimkel.

Crowds gathered at the corner to watch the mountain forming. Police sirens could be heard. The mountain kept growing higher. Mountain climbers with spiked boots were starting to gather at the bottom.

"Hey!" they shouted to each other. "Let's go climb Shaymess Mountain!"

Just then, Rabbi Heller came back from the *Bais*

Medrash where he had been studying *Daf Yomi*. He stopped short when he saw the mountain.

"Oh, my goodness," he cried. "This mountain will cost me a million dollars!"

Two burly policeman came out of a yellow patrol car.

"Hey, whose mountain is this?" they wanted to know. "You're blocking traffic."

To make matters worse, Cantor Chirenboim suddenly appeared with a half dozen scratched cantorial records.

"Could I throw these in also?" he asked. "Boi, boi, boi, boi. Bum, dum, dee dum."

"Chaimkel, what have you done?" cried Rabbi Heller. "Look at that mountain!"

Everyone looked up at the same time. In the blue, golden glistening Canadian summer sky stood a beautiful mountain of *shaymess*, snow-capped like Mount Hermon. For a second, there was absolute stillness and beauty.

And then it happened. From the very top, one carton started to tumble down, and then another, and then another. A scream went up from the crowd.

"Shaymess Mountain is falling! Run, everyone! The whole city of Toronto is going to be drowned in *shaymess*!"

There was the roar of falling and smashing, and people ran helter skelter in every direction as *sefer* after *sefer* came crashing down.

"Let me out of here!" screamed Chaimkel, and he

rushed to escape through the brown *Yehoshua* door, trying to dodge the flying *sefarim*.

"Say *Modeh Ahnee*, Chaimkel," his father shook him awake. "Say *Modeh Ahnee*. It's a new day."

Chaimkel opened his eyes and looked up. No *sefarim*. Just the bottom of his brother's bunk bed.

The next morning, Chaimkel was relieved to see that there was no mountain at Sefer-Tov. Rabbi Heller's plan had worked.

During the night he had posted a large sign in the Sefer-Tov window:

NO MORE
SHAYMESS
PLEASE!!

He had also put up signs in a few *shuls* and stores asking people to stop bringing in used *sefarim*.

"Don't worry, Chaimkel," Rabbi Heller reassured Chaimkel, who felt bad about all the trouble he had caused. "You can only learn by making mistakes."

"But it's going to cost you five hundred dollars, *Abba*!"

Rabbi Heller smiled sadly.

"Well, if it costs, it costs," he said. "What we earn is up to the *Ribono Shel Olam*, not us. If it means we lose five hundred dollars, that's what the *Ribono Shel Olam* wanted; it's a *kaporah*. We mustn't complain."

"When are they going to take away the cartons?" asked Chaimkel.

"I arranged with the *gabbai* of Congregation Beth Midabrim for a truck to come at three o'clock. He agreed that we could pay off the fee at a few dollars a month."

In his heart, Chaimkel promised he would somehow help his father pay off the amount.

It was a warm, quiet day. Just a customer or two slipped in. It was almost three o'clock when a short, plain looking man came into the store, quietly poking around here and there.

"Can I help you?" asked Rabbi Heller, looking up from his *Daf Yomi*.

"I heard you have some used *sefarim*," the man said quietly. "Could I please take a look at them?"

"Used *sefarim*?" chuckled Rabbi Heller. "I'll show you used *sefarim*."

He thought the man would appreciate the joke of seeing that the used *sefarim* were really tattered *shaymess*.

Chaimkel understood and opened one of the cartons. They expected the man to look up puzzled. Or to laugh. But he didn't. Instead, he started examining the books in an orderly fashion, checking the covers and stacking loose pages.

"Do you have more in the other cartons?" he asked.

Chaimkel and his father looked at each other.

"More? Yes, cartons of them," said Rabbi Heller quickly. "Look over here. I'll show you."

The man sifted through a few more cartons. Finally, he brushed the dust off his fingers and turned to Rabbi

Heller, excitement in his eyes.

"Priceless!" he exclaimed.

"I beg your pardon," said Rabbi Heller, puzzled.

"These books are priceless," said the man.

"But they're just *shaymess*," said Rabbi Heller.

"Well, the pages may be *shaymess*, but the covers are full of stamps and signatures from some of the oldest, most famous names in Toronto. You have Toronto history in these covers. May I make you an offer for your collection?"

"An offer!!??"

"Yes. Would a thousand dollars be satisfactory?"

"A what?" squealed Chaimkel.

"Quiet, sonny," said the man, patting Chaimkel on his dusty *yarmulke*. "Yes, a thousand dollars. I am sure my committee would be happy to pay a thousand dollars for this *shaymess*. And any others you may have. Is that satisfactory?"

"S-s-satisfactory!?" stammered Rabbi Heller, a stunned expression on his face. "Why, that's incredible! Wonderful! *Baruch Hashem*! I can hardly believe it! But one thing. Will they be properly cared for?"

"Absolutely!" the man promised. "Whatever we can't use in our files will be buried according to *Halachah* at Mount Hermon Cemetery. Everything will be treated with great respect."

There were little blue stars in Chaimkel's eyes. One thousand dollars! The Chaimkel (and Shulamis) Used *Sefer* and Book Department had made more money than Sefer-Tov had all month! The deal was struck.

That night, there was a great celebration in the Heller household. Everyone was happy and thankful to Hashem. Baruch got an extra cookie. Chaimkel bought a new *yarmulke*. Happiest of all was Shulamis, who was once again a partner.

Rabbi Heller *davened* with special thankfulness that night. Sefer-Tov had been given a new lease on life.

Chapter Six

The Esrog Without Mazel

ONCE EVERY YEAR, SEFER-TOV became too small. Customers streamed in one after another, crowded around each other, pressed to make their purchases.

It was the *esrog* season.

Chaimkel and Shulamis helped Rabbi Heller arrange all his *esrogim* neatly in boxes, the prices marked clearly. Like little yellow soldiers, the *esrogim* presented themselves to the buyers. Some were short and stout, others tall and regal. Some were still lime-green, others pale yellow and still others ripe and deep colored.

There was a great parade of customers. The *esrogim* sat on the shelves of a central island, while the customers marched around and around, peering here, touching here, squinting there. In Rabbi Heller's back office, there were more, still unopened boxes.

Each day, buyers came and took one, two, even three and four *esrog* sets.

"For me, for Uncle Zalman, for Benny and for my brother-in-law who's coming from Monsey."

They all walked out happy.

It was busy. Chaimkel bound up the *lulavim*. Shulamis wrote down the sales and made a record of who took on credit. From time to time, the *yeshiva* boys who helped went with Rabbi Heller to cut fresh *aravos* from Rabbi Rubin's *aravah* bush. Rabbi Heller ran back and forth in the store, giving advice, thanking everyone for buying, humming a *niggun* under his breath as he figured out how he would pay his creditors. It was a happy time.

Every few days, Rabbi Heller drove to the airport to pick up new supplies of *lulavim* and *esrogim*. Often, *shuls* and schools added to their earlier orders. The store stayed open and crowded until eleven or sometimes twelve o'clock.

Each night, the family came home exhausted from a long day. "*Baruch Hashem*," Rabbi Heller would say. "I think we'll make it to *Pesach* again."

After a few days, however, a frown began to form on

86

Rabbi Heller's brow. Sales were brisk as customers impressed by Sefer-Tov's honesty piled in, and yet, something was wrong.

One night, a few days before *Sukkos*, Rachel Heller decided to say something. The children were in their pajamas, ready to go to sleep.

"Everything is so fine," she said as she passed her husband a cup of tea. "Why the long face?"

"There is one *esrog* I bought for more than fifty dollars. To me, it seems to be a *mehudar*, beautiful, clean, nicely formed. And yet, no one wants to buy it. They bring it to the window, look at it, twirl it around. But it's always the same. They put it back. I'm afraid we may get stuck with it."

"Don't worry," his wife reassured him. "Hashem will help. I'm sure you'll find a customer for it."

"I guess so," agreed Rabbi Heller. "But somehow, it bothers me."

The children went to bed and fell asleep quickly. Everyone, that is, except Chaimkel. It bothered him, too. Imagine, an *esrog* no one would buy!

He promised himself to keep an eye out for it.

The next day, Chaimkel asked his father to show him the *esrog*.

"Here it is, Chaimkel!" said Rabbi Heller.

He opened the white, cardboard box carefully, unwrapped the material in which the *esrog* was packed and took out the *esrog*. Chaimkel gently lifted it and held it near the window.

"It looks nice to me," said Chaimkel. He had become

a bit of a *maven* in the past few days.

"Yes," agreed Rabbi Heller, carefully returning it. "But it seems to be an *esrog* that doesn't have any *mazel*. No one wants it."

By eleven o'clock, Sefer-Tov was crowded again. Rabbi Gorman came in, a warm wide smile on his face. Mr. Silverstein bought an *esrog* for his brother-in-law.

In the early afternoon, a well dressed gentleman walked in and began marching around the island, poking through the boxes. He stopped at the *esrog* without *mazel* and lifted it up. Chaimkel closed in on him.

"Nice *esrog*, isn't it?" asked Chaimkel.

"Not bad," the man sniffed.

"Beautiful *giddel*," Chaimkel said, describing the shape.

"I've seen better, I've seen worse," the man answered coolly. "I'll look further, but I'll hold on to it for the meantime. Set it aside for me, would you?"

Hopefully, Chaimkel took the *esrog* without *mazel* and set it on a reserve shelf.

"Don't worry," he whispered. "Your *mazel* will change. I'll get you sold yet."

In a few minutes, the man was back. He held a second *esrog* in his hand.

"I found this *esrog* which is fa-a-ar from perfect. And then there's the other *esrog* you set aside for me. Let me see it again."

The man held an *esrog* in each hand and compared them. Chaimkel's heart leaped. His *esrog* without *mazel* was much nicer. Surely, it would be chosen!

"Do me a favor, Rabbi Heller," the man said. "Let me take these home for about an hour. I want to study them in a special light, then I'll make my decision."

Rabbi Heller and Chaimkel looked at each other, thinking the same thing. There was no contest! The *esrog* without *mazel* would win hands down.

"Certainly," Rabbi Heller agreed.

The man took both *esrogim* and left.

"*Baruch Hashem*," said Chaimkel. "I'm sure it'll go."

His father remained silent.

Two hours later, the man returned. There was a pleased smile on his face.

"I've chosen," he announced. "One I really like."

"Which one?" Chaimkel and his father asked together, so loudly that everyone in the store stopped and stared at them.

"Which one?" Rabbi Heller asked more quietly.

"Hmmph," said the man, not liking all the attention. "This one."

He opened the box with the other *esrog*.

Chaimkel couldn't restrain himself.

"But the other *esrog* is so much nicer!"

The man took out the *esrog* without *mazel* and showed it to Chaimkel.

"I don't like the *pitum*," he said.

"The *pitum*!" exclaimed Chaimkel. "This *pitum* is beautiful, straight and balanced!"

"It's crooked," the man insisted.

Chaimkel's eyes opened wide.

"How could you say it's crooked when it's straight?"

asked Chaimkel, visibly upset.

"Listen, young fellow," said the man. "I'm buying the *esrog*, and I'm paying for it. I say it's crooked."

Rabbi Heller gave Chaimkel a sharp look. The man had a right to buy what he wanted. Chaimkel took the *esrog* without *mazel* and walked off, extremely upset. He held the *esrog* in front of him and addressed it.

"*Esrog*, I say you are beautiful. Don't worry, we'll get you sold off yet!"

The next day, the *esrog* parade continued. The great stack of *esrog* boxes in the back office was shrinking, and Rabbi Heller looked happier and happier. It seemed there would even be something left over for savings.

Just one sad thought remained. The *esrog* without *mazel* just wasn't being sold. People stopped by, nodded their heads and admired it, but in the end, they always chose another *esrog*. And they gave all sorts of reasons.

"It's cheaper."

"It's straighter."

"This *esrog* reminds me of my Uncle Feivish."

"It's nice, but . . ."

And they left it there, unwanted.

From time to time, Chaimkel stopped by the *esrog*, clutching at the *lulav* he was tying, and whispered, "Don't worry *esrog* without *mazel*, we'll get you sold yet!"

Later that day, the store was noisy with buyers. Suddenly, a hush fell in the room.

Mr. Oliphant had entered Sefer-Tov.

Rabbi Heller was surprised to see the fabulously wealthy manufacturer in his tiny little Sefer-Tov.

The great industrialist surveyed the store, waiting for service. He did not care to join the rowdy march around the *esrog* island. The other customers nodded to him respectfully. Mr. Oliphant was in the store!

Rabbi Heller ran over to him.

"*Shalom Aleichem*, Mr. Oliphant," he said.

Chaimkel could tell his father was nervous. Such an important person, written up in all the newspapers, to be in his store!

Mr. Oliphant nodded and shook hands coolly.

"Do you have *esrogim*?" he asked.

Rabbi Heller was so startled he was speechless for a moment. Chaimkel fumed inwardly. What did Mr. Oliphant think everyone was doing, buying pickles?

"Why, of course," Rabbi Heller finally answered.

"I would like to see something nice," said Mr. Oliphant. "But really nice! You understand? Nice!"

Chaimkel was fascinated. Mr. Oliphant had thick eyebrows, streaked with little silver hairs. Every time he said the word "nice," his little silver hairs lifted, like the sound gauge on a tape recorder.

"I will go and look myself," said Rabbi Heller. "I will go to the back office and see what I can find special."

Rabbi Heller ran back inside, but Chaimkel had his own plans. He knew that everyone in the city would be watching the *esrog* that Mr. Oliphant, chairman of ten corporations, would purchase.

"Ahem, may I show you an *esrog*, Mr. Oliphant?" asked Chaimkel.

The little silver hairs went up immediately. Chaimkel knew what was coming.

"Is it nice?" asked Mr. Oliphant.

"Very nice," answered Chaimkel, lifting his little red eyebrows in response. He ran to the *esrog* without *mazel*. He kissed it and whispered, "Your luck is going to change now!"

He gently carried the *esrog* to Mr. Oliphant. At that moment, his father was rushing over with two more *esrogim*.

"Here, Mr. Oliphant," Rabbi Heller said. "Have a look at these."

"Wait," Mr. Oliphant lifted an eyebrow. "I want to take a look at the *esrog* your son just brought me."

Rabbi Heller looked at Chaimkel, and their eyes met for a second. Chaimkel gave the barest, knowing nod to his father.

Mr. Oliphant was impressed by Chaimkel's choice. His mouth pursed, his silver streaked eyebrows arched higher and higher. He touched the little *pitum* with the tip of his little finger.

"Not bad at all," he finally spoke. "May I take it to a better light?"

Chaimkel's heart raced with joy.

"Of course, of course," said Rabbi Heller. "Bring it to the window, please."

The three of them marched to the window under the watchful eyes of everyone in the store.

Mr. Oliphant stared at the *esrog* for a long time, turning and turning and turning it in his hand. He looked like he was studying the map of the world.

Finally, he looked up and turned to Chaimkel.

"No," he said.

"No?" breathed Chaimkel, barely able to speak.

"No," repeated Mr. Oliphant. "Here, let me show you, young man." His little finger drifted over the side of the *esrog*. "You see how it's shaped? It's a little bit too overweight. You see how heavy it looks on the bottom? An *esrog* should be like a tower."

"But it is like a tower!" insisted Chaimkel. "It's tall and even and lovely."

"Lovely?" said Mr. Oliphant. "Yes, lovely. But still, it's just a little too wide on the bottom. I'm willing to pay anything, but I want it perfect!"

He returned the *esrog* to Chaimkel. Chaimkel knew there was no arguing with the great man. Sadly, he put back the *esrog*. In the end, Mr. Oliphant walked out without buying anything.

That night, Chaimkel tossed and turned in his bed. He was overtired and overexcited, running back and forth all day with the *esrogim*, tying up *lulavim*, running to cut more and more *aravos*.

He said the *Shema* and *Rigzu* and tried to fall asleep, but he couldn't.

He thought about the *esrogim*, and imagined where in Eretz Yisrael they grew. He saw the *esrog* without *mazel*, large and golden like a pumpkin door, its *pitum* rising like an arch.

He knocked on the *esrog* door, and it swung open. What world was this?

There were hundreds of *esrogim* scurrying around on little green legs. They all crowded into the store.

Chaimkel tapped one on the shoulder.

"Where's everyone rushing to?" he asked.

"It's almost *Sukkos*," the *esrog* answered impatiently. "We have to pick out an owner for *Yom Tov*."

The *esrogim* formed a vast circle parade, as they looked over the *baalei batim* they should go to. They were all there, all the customers who had been in Sefer-Tov looking for *esrogim*.

Two *esrogim* looked over a customer. They clasped their green little arms behind their backs and exchanged opinions.

"What do you think?" asked one.

The second *esrog* eyed the man closely.

"Too overweight," he said. "Looks to me he does more *chulent* eating than Torah studying."

They moved on. There was a handsome, tanned young man, looking hopeful.

"Hmphh, not too bad," nodded one of the *esrogim*, "but too suntanned. You don't get such a suntan in a *Bais Medrash*."

And so it went, a noisy crowd of *esrogim* who looked over the stock of customers. Chaimkel recognized one of the *esrogim* as his friend, the *esrog* without *mazel*.

"How is it going?" asked Chaimkel.

"No luck yet," said the *esrog*.

A friend of the *esrog* without *mazel* came over.

"I think I found something for you. Come, take a look."

Chaimkel followed the *esrog*. Sure enough, there was the well-dressed man in the camel hair coat. The *esrog* looked him over from head to foot. The man straightened his tie and adjusted his handkerchief.

"Not bad," said the *esrog* without *mazel*. "But let me take a closer look at him outside."

A few *esrogim* carried the distinguished looking man outside. He was eager to be chosen. Chaimkel followed, and they all stood outside Sefer-Tov.

"Well, what do you think?" asked the store owner. The camel-hair coated man practically glowed.

"I've seen a lot worse," said the *esrog* without *mazel*. "But . . . But . . ."

"But what?"

"His nose is crooked."

"What?"

"His nose is crooked. Look, you see it is out of joint. I know *baalei batim*, and I'm telling you there's something not right about that nose."

The man in the camel hair coat turned pale.

"My nose is on right!" he protested. "I've had this nose for years. It is a beautiful nose, a distinguished nose."

"Yes," answered the *esrog* quickly. "But you seem to have held it so long in the air that it got twisted out of shape."

"I have a wonderfully straight nose," shouted the man. "How dare you criticize my nose!"

"Listen," said the *esrog* flatly. "It's my money. When I say a nose is not straight, it's not straight. Back to the shelf with you."

Chaimkel slipped back into the store. What a commotion! He followed the *esrogim* as they paraded around and around and around the *baalei batim*.

"I'll take Reb Velvel!" said one *esrog*, plucking up a nice old rabbi.

"Give me that computer operator," shouted another, elbowing in with little green pipe stem arms. "He learns Torah in the afternoon after work."

"I'll take the store owner," decided another *esrog* happily. "Not a great scholar, but very honest."

And so they went, *esrog* after *esrog*, picking out a *baal habayis* who was worthy.

"Hey, *rabbosai*, what about this one?" announced the store owner proudly. "I have a beautiful one here. Take a look at this *mehudar*!"

The *esrogim* stopped and stared. Chaimkel looked. It was Mr. Oliphant!

"Wow!" shouted the *esrogim*. "That's a *sheiner baal habayis* if we ever saw one!"

"Look at that color!"

"I like that Italian hat!" said another.

"He'll cost a lot, but it's worth it," cautioned the owner.

In walked the *esrog* without *mazel*.

"Let me see a really nice *baal habayis*," he demanded.

"This one is just for you," the owner rushed over. "Just brought out from the back room." He handed over Mr. Oliphant to the *esrog*.

Mr. Oliphant looked at the *esrog*, and the *esrog* looked at him.

"Very impressive," said the *esrog*. "Come to the window. I want a better look."

A few of his *esrog* friends joined him. Mr. Oliphant's silver flecked eyebrows bobbed up and down happily, and the *esrogim* made admiring remarks.

"Known all over . . ."

"Made a large donation recently . . ."

"Occasionally opens a *sefer* . . ."

The store owner beamed proudly.

Finally, the *esrog* made up its mind.

"No," he said.

"No?" cried Mr. Oliphant, shocked. "Why not? Look at my list of credits."

"Very nice," said the *esrog* without *mazel*. "But you're a little too heavy on the bottom. You're uneven. Compared to what you have, you haven't given enough, haven't given quietly enough and haven't given sweetly enough. Always with a grumph and harumph. You're too weighted down on the bottom, too many bank-books, stocks and bonds."

"But look at me!" Mr. Oliphant spluttered. "Look at this shape!"

"Nice, nice," admitted the *esrog*. "But still could be better. For a top-dollar I want a top *baal habayis*. I mean a real *baal habayis*. Perfecto!"

Mr. Oliphant returned to his place. Chaimkel began to tremble uncomfortably.

"I must leave this *esrog* store," he said. "The whole place is shaking. I must get out."

He rushed out of the store like in a dream, back out quick through the *esrog* door. Baruch was shaking him awake.

"Get up, get up, sleepy head," Baruch insisted.

Groggily, Chaimkel opened one eye. It was the day before *Sukkos*.

There had never been a day like that at Sefer-Tov.

All the people who left their *esrog* buying for the last minute descended on the store. It was almost impossible to get in. The other stores had run out of *esrogim*, and there was only one store left. Sefer-Tov.

"Wheeeee!!" sang Chaimkel to himself.

Luckily, his father had ordered a last minute shipment from New York. Every so often, Chaimkel jumped into the car with a *yeshiva* student and went to cut more *aravos*.

"*Baruch Hashem, Baruch Hashem,*" Rabbi Heller whispered over and over to himself. "There was a great *berachah* this year." His reputation for not overcharging customers had brought a blessing to Sefer-Tov.

By late afternoon, all the *esrogim* were completely gone. The last customer slipped his *lulav* into the plastic bag, shook hands with Rabbi Heller and left. The floor was littered with *aravos* leaves and pieces of *lulav* leaves.

"I can't believe it! I can't believe it!" Rabbi Heller told his wife over the phone. "Every *esrog* sold. One second." He made change for a small child who bought a last minute *Sukkah* poster. "We may even be able to save a little towards a house. Wait a minute. What is it, Chaimkel?"

Chaimkel had run over to his father. His face was white.

"*Abba*, the *esrog*!" he cried. "It's still here!"

Rabbi Heller looked up.

"The *esrog*?" he asked. "Which *esrog*?"

"The *esrog* without *mazel*," said Chaimkel. "Someone must have stuffed it on a high book shelf and not returned it. It was never sold."

"I'll call you back later," said Rabbi Heller into the phone and hung it up. "But you told me it had been sold, Chaimkel. You told me someone had taken it. You were so happy!"

"I thought so, *Abba*," said Chaimkel. "One minute it was on the shelf, and the next minute it was gone. I thought someone had grabbed it and paid at the counter."

Rabbi Heller was upset.

"No one will buy it now," he said forlornly. "Forty eight U.S. dollars out the window. Besides . . ." He picked up the *esrog* and turned it around and around. "Besides, it's not fair. Every single *esrog* in Toronto was sold except this one. And it is so beautiful!"

"Why do you think Hashem allowed that?" asked Chaimkel, who was near tears. He had even dreamed about the *esrog*, it meant so much to him.

"Who knows?" sighed Rabbi Heller. "Everything and everyone needs *mazel*. Even a *Sefer Torah* in the

Aron Hakodesh needs *mazel.* And if you don't have *mazel*, then . . ."

"Then what?"

"Then, it's bitter."

They were still staring glumly at the *esrog* without *mazel* when the door opened and a head appeared in the doorway. Avraham Gólding slipped into the store.

"Are you still open?" he asked timidly.

"Of course," said Rabbi Heller. "Come in. What can I do for you?"

"Could I use your washroom?"

"Of course," answered Rabbi Heller.

Avraham set down his heavy packages and quickly headed for the back. He opened the door.

"No, no, Avraham," said Rabbi Heller. "That's the closet."

Avraham Golding mumbled his apologies and disappeared into the washroom. A few minutes later, he reappeared and picked up his packages.

"Thank you," he mumbled and headed out.

"One second," said Rabbi Heller: "Not so fast. How does it go with you, Avraham?"

Avraham Golding owned a clothing store that had gone bankrupt.

"*Baruch Hashem*," he mumbled downcast. "We are healthy, but it is not easy. You understand." Mr. Golding had five young children.

"I understand," said Rabbi Heller. "Why didn't you buy an *esrog* from me this year?"

The question brought a frightening result. Mr.

Golding dropped his packages and began weeping like a child. He reached for a tissue.

"You want to know how I am?" he wailed. "Miserable, that's how! You ask me why I don't buy an *esrog*? It's a miracle I have enough to feed my children and meet my mortgage payments. My wife and I fight constantly about money, and my children are not learning the way they should. *Esrog*!? I didn't even buy myself shoe laces for *Yom Tov*."

Rabbi Heller looked away. Chaimkel knew his father was crying. He felt like bawling himself. Mr. Golding lifted his heavy bags and gave Chaimkel a reassuring little smile.

"I must go," he said. "Have a good *Yom Tov*."

"Wait!" Rabbi Heller shouted. "Avraham, please do me a favor."

Quickly, he took the *esrog* without *mazel* and handed it to Mr. Golding Without *Mazel*.

"You need an *esrog*, and the *esrog* needs a *baal babayis*," he said. "Take it, and may both your *mazels* change for the better."

"But I can't take it for nothing," Mr. Golding protested.

"Do you have eighteen cents?" asked Rabbi Heller.

"Eighteen cents? For a ninety dollar esrog?"

"It's eighteen cents more than I expected to get for it," said Rabbi Heller. "Don't you see? This *esrog* was waiting for you."

Mr. Golding fished in his pocket for eighteen cents, and in a few minutes, he walked out with one of the most beautiful *esrogim* in Toronto. He was beaming.

Rabbi Heller shut the lights in the store and started locking up. Chaimkel's eyes met his father's for a second, and they both smiled.

"It's going to be a nice *Yom Tov*," said Rabbi Heller.

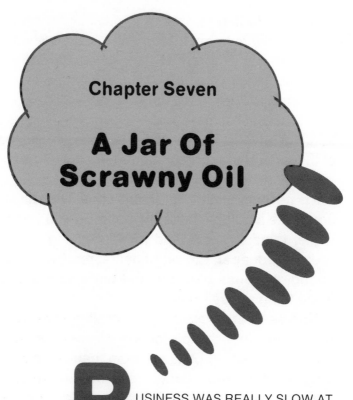

Chapter Seven

A Jar Of Scrawny Oil

BUSINESS WAS REALLY SLOW AT Sefer-Tov. It was the *Cheshvan* slump—after the *esrogim* and before the *Chanukah* season. Rabbi Heller sat in the store together with Shulamis and Chaimkel, looking out the window for customers.

"Will anyone ever show up?" asked Chaimkel. "Where is everyone?"

"I know," grumbled Shulamis. "Shopping at—"

"Shulamis!" Rabbi Heller shushed her. "The owner of the other book store also has to make a living.

Whatever Hashem wants us to make, we'll make."

"But will it ever get busy again?" asked Shulamis.

"I hope so," answered Rabbi Heller worriedly.

"*Abba*," said Chaimkel. "Do you know any good *Chanukah* stories to tell us while we wait?"

Just at that moment, Rabbi Heller was setting up a bottle of olive oil for the *Chanukah* display. He looked at the jar and thought for a moment.

"Yes, I do. Let's all sit down."

It is never bitter cold in Eretz Yisrael. The sun shines down like a golden flame, shimmering and warm. The winter rains soak the land with life-giving water. The roots dig deeper, the branches spread wider. In the spring, the buds blossom, the birds sing and every living thing praises Hashem.

No trees were prouder than the olive trees, because they knew that the oil for the *Menorah* in the *Bais Hamikdash* would be taken from them. And of all the olive trees in Eretz Yisrael, none were more beautiful than the trees in the small Galilean village of Tekoah.

"There are no trees like us in all of Eretz Yisrael," they boasted.

One tree in particular was famous for its wonderful olives. It was old and full of knots, with a thick trunk so round that three children standing around it could hardly touch hands. No one knew how long it had stood there, but the pure mountain sunlight, the nearby brook and the abundant rains made its olives so full they practically dripped with oil.

If that was not enough, behind it was the beautiful

stone wall of an ancient *shul*, which made each silvery and ripening olive stand out.

In the spring, when the first olive buds appeared, all the children went out, formed a great circle around the tree and sang. The olives on the trees grew heavier and greener each day. The whole neighborhood bore the tangy scent of fresh olive oil.

"Who is like us?" cried the uppermost olives in the tree as they turned their shining faces to the sun. "Who is purer and more beautiful? Soon, the *Kohain Gadol* will use us to light up the *Bais Hamikdash*!"

But not all the olives on the tree were so happy.

The olives on the lowest branches were blocked off from direct sunlight, and the olives that faced the old *shul* wall had even less sunlight and rain. These olives tried to soak in as much sunlight as possible, but almost all of it went to the olives on top. These other olives grew very slowly, and their oil was far from the best.

The fat, rich olives on top looked down at their skinnier brothers and snickered.

"Poor things down there," they taunted. "How do you ever expect to make it to the *Bais Hamikdash*? I am afraid you will wind up in someone's *latkes*. That's all you're fit for!"

"We still have time," answered the undernourished olives. "Maybe we can still make it."

The upper olives with their suntanned faces looked down.

"Don't fool yourself," they said. "Be realistic. Who do

you think will be chosen for the *Menorah*, our beautiful oil or your skinny little drops?"

The skinny olives below turned toward the wall, hid their pale faces and prayed. "Hashem," they pleaded. "We also want to serve You."

One morning, the *Gizbar* of the *Bais Hamikdash* appeared. He was the official in charge of checking all the olive trees in Eretz Yisrael and picking the finest olives for the *Menorah*. He knew where to go—straight to Tekoah.

When the townspeople heard he was coming, they all went out to greet him. They prepared a great table laden with fruits, cakes and wine. The *Gizbar* made a *berachah*, tasted something and then announced, "It is time to choose olives for the *Menorah*!"

Led by the *Gizbar* in his fine robes, the whole town walked straight to the beautiful old tree near the stone wall. Each sun-drenched olive beautified and twisted itself until it almost glittered. A little drop of dew glistened here and there from a handsome, green brow. The *Gizbar* stretched out his arms in sheer joy.

"Are there more beautiful olives in all the world than the olives of this old Tekoah tree?" he exclaimed. "I declare that these fat, ripe beauties will make oil for the *Menorah* itself!"

The *Gizbar's* assistant tapped him respectfully on the shoulder. "What about those pale, scrawny ones on the bottom branches?" he asked.

The *Gizbar* gave them a quick glance. He fingered one or two between his fingers, squinched up his nose and put them back down.

"No, those you can forget about," he said. "Maybe we'll take just a few. It's the beautiful ones on top I'm after. These others are just not good enough."

The top olives peered down, winked and laughed. "We told you not to bother!" they crowed. "You're just not good enough!"

The bottom olives were silent with shame. They turned their pale faces to the *shul* wall. "Hashem," they whispered. "Whatever is Your Will, that is what we accept."

All day, the pickers combed through the great tree, plucking olive after olive like precious gems. The chosen olives were gently placed into a large basket to be brought to the pressing house and squeezed into oil.

But a mistake was made. One of the olive pickers plucked some of the scrawny olives and threw them in together with the fat olives.

"We don't want them!" screamed the fat olives. "They don't belong with us!"

The scrawny olives did not answer. "Whatever You want, Hashem," they just whispered.

No one heard the protests of the fat olives, and the poor pale olives were carried off along with the rest.

The pressing house had a large noisy room. There were two grindstones in the center that crushed and squeezed the olives by the thousands until the oil poured out like a river. But that is not where these precious olives were headed.

"Olives to make oil for the *Menorah*!" announced the *Gizbar*.

All the workers greeted the basket with rejoicing and song.

"There is some mistake!" shouted the fat olives over the rim of the basket. "You've mixed in some lower-class olives. Ohhhh!!"

Like a small waterfall, the basket of olives was poured into a stone dish. No great grindstones for these special *Menorah* olives. Carefully and gently, the *Gizbar's* assistant began squeezing the rich drops of oil from each olive.

The almost pure olive oil floated to the top, with a tiny bit of pulp still mixed in. Then, it was poured down the sides of wicker baskets.

Drip . . . drip . . . drip.

Drop by drop, the finest, clearest oil in all Eretz Yisrael flowed out. Perfect, spotless, holy. Quickly, it was poured into small earthen vessels and sealed tight.

"But there is some mistake here!" screamed the jars filled with the oil from the fat, beautiful olives. "Look! One jar is filled with oil from those scrawny, pitiful olives. They don't belong with us!"

"They will ruin our reputation!" cried another fine jar.

"They're not in our oily social class!" clamored yet another jar. "Get us away from them. Put them somewhere else."

Again, it was too late. The jars had been sealed. No one could hear their complaints. A fine golden box lined with purple silk was prepared, and all the jars were placed neatly inside.

"*Baruch hashem*, we've gotten this far," the jar of skinny olive oil whispered hopefully. "Whatever Hashem wants!"

For days and days, the jars of oil traveled by wagon to Yerushalayim, down the Galilean mountains, along the sandy coast of the Great Sea and back up the Hills of Yehudah. They entered proudly through the Western Gate of the holy city.

"Make way!" everyone shouted. "Make way for the holy oil of the *Menorah*!"

The *Gizbar* greeted his assistant at the entrance to the *Bais Hamikdash*.

"Do you have the oil?" he asked. "Is it ready?"

Proudly, the assistant whipped out the jars and laid them on a golden tray, one by one. The *Gizbar* lifted a few, uncorked them and peered at the contents.

"Wonderful! Beautiful!" he exclaimed happily. "I will bring them straight to the *Kohain Gadol*!"

"Pssst! *Gizbar*! Hey, *Gizbar*! Wait a minute!" the fine oil jars whispered excitedly. "There's been a mistake. One of the jars doesn't belong here. Pssst! *Gizbar*, quick! Look over there!"

But the *Gizbar* was so excited he didn't notice them. He carried the tray straight to the *Kohain Gadol* sitting in his great stone chamber.

"For the *Menorah*!" announced the *Gizbar* with pride.

The *Kohain Gadol*, his long beard flowing white over

the tops of the jars, peered at the fine oil in front of him.

"May you burn brightly in honor of Hashem and His Torah!" he prayed. "May you cast a holy light over all Yisrael!"

Very carefully and with great love, he stamped his seal on each jug: "*Kadosh l'Menorah*."

"*Baruch Hashem*, that we've reached this point," said the oil from the scrawny olives.

With a squish, the *Kohain Gadol* inscribed his seal on this jar of oil, too.

"You don't belong with us!" yelled a jar of fine oil at the scrawny one. "How dare you allow yourself to be included."

"It's an absolute disgrace!" cried a second fine jar.

"Who ever heard of such a scandal!" cried a third.

The jar of scrawny oil tried to answer back.

"But this is what Hashem desires," it insisted. "We did not pick ourselves or squeeze ourselves or seal ourselves. And after all, we'll only burn for one night. Please leave us alone."

"You don't belong to our group!" the biggest, finest jug answered firmly. "You have no right to be here."

Meanwhile, the *Gizbar* joyously carried the golden tray laden with the jars into the chamber of oil. He put the tray on a shelf and left.

At last, the jugs of fine oil saw their chance. The single jar of scrawny oil was at the edge.

"Here's our chance, fellows," the jars of fine oil whispered to each other.

Suddenly, they all pushed in one direction. The poor

jar of oil was knocked off the tray and rolled off.

"We've done it!" the jars screamed happily. "We got rid of the intruder once and for all."

Over and over, the poor jar rolled.

"Help us! Help us!" it cried.

It spun and slipped and flipped until it fell into a crack in the floor. There was a little notch under the stone, pitch black and hidden. There it stopped.

"Oh, no," cried the jar of scrawny oil. "No one will ever find us now. Never! But if that is what You want, Hashem, that is for the best, too."

Some time later, a great war erupted. The wicked Greeks captured the city of Yerushalayim. Thousands and thousands of soldiers, with long spears, sharp swords, ladders, torches, helmets and shields, gathered at the doors of the *Bais Hamikdash*.

"This is the Holy Temple of the Jews!" they shouted. "Break down the doors, boys. Knock down the doors! Set fire to the walls! Kill the priests!"

"Are you ready, boys?" shouted one of the generals.

"Ready!" they yelled back.

"Shall we attack, boys?!"

"Attack! Attack!" they shouted back.

"Get ready!" commanded the general. "Steady! Attaaack!!"

Like the sea swamping a broken wall, they swarmed in by the thousands. The Jewish defenders and *Kohanim* begged for mercy, but the soldiers were pitiless. The poor *Kohanim* fell at the foot of the *Mizbayach*. Fires burned everywhere.

It was over in a short while. The Greeks gathered in the central courtyard. They were all smiles.

"The Temple is in our hands, boys!" announced the general. "You've done a good day's work. Congratulations!"

"Hurray!" they thundered in response.

"I say we have a party!" shouted one of the officers. "An oil and wine party! We'll rub ourselves down with their finest holy oils and drink up their holy wine."

"Great idea!" said the general. "We've certainly earned it."

"Wow!" screamed the soldiers with excitement. "What we always wanted. An oil and wine party!"

The thousands of soldiers fanned out among the hundreds of chambers, rooms and closets in the *Bais Hamikdash*. The first door they broke down was the chamber of oil .The precious jars of oil were just taking their afternoon nap when the door was broken open, and hands were laid on them. And the very first jars taken were the jars of fine oils marked "*Kadosh l'Menorah*" with the *Kohain Gadol's* seal.

"Wait! Wait!" they screamed frantically. "You are no *Kohanim*! Where are you taking us? We are the finest oil in Eretz Yisrael! We are supposed to burn in the *Menorah*!"

"You'll rub down my back, not the *Menorah*," the soldier holding them yelled.

"We have connections here!" shouted another jar angrily. "You can't take—"

The soldier angrily smashed the jar against the wall,

and it lay quietly, its oil oozing out.

The soldier distributed the jars among his friends. The oils suddenly realized there was nothing they could do. They would all be made *tamai*, impure. Just before they disappeared, they lifted up their tops to Hashem. "Did we do something wrong, Hashem?" they pleaded. But it was too late.

Only one jar of oil had escaped. The jar of scrawny oil was still hidden in the little dark hole.

Terrible days followed during which the enemy controlled Yerushalayim, but Hashem listened to the desperate prayers of the Jews. Brave soldiers came forward who held a *Siddur* in one hand and a sword in the other. They fought and fought, just a few valiant men against great armies.

"We have the soldiers!" crowed the Greeks.

"We have the Torah," answered the Jews.

"We have huge swords and spears!" taunted the Greeks.

"But we have a *Chumash* and *Tehillim*!" answered the Jews.

"We will come with all our armies," shouted the Greeks. "Tens of thousands!"

"But we will come with one Hashem, who is greater!" the Jews retorted.

The Jews attacked again and again, at night, in the mountains, shocking, tricking, confusing. Soon, Yerushalayim was again in the hands of the Jews, and they stood at the mighty gates of the *Bais Hamikdash*.

"We have come back!" they announced happily.

116

But when they pushed open the great gates and looked inside, they could not even speak. They sat down and cried. The beautiful, holy *Bais Hamikdash* had been turned inside out. Broken jars and vessels littered the ground.

The *Kohanim* walked through the grounds and saw how everything had been desecrated. They climbed the steps to the *Heichal* sanctuary. The golden *Menorah* was dark and cold.

"We will make you bright again!" they promised.

They looked at each other.

"Oil!" they cried. "We need oil for the *Menorah*! We will light it again. Tonight!"

It was *Kislev*, and a chill wind blew.

"Oil, *rabbosai*!" a *Kohain* called out from the steps of the courtyard. "We must find holy oil, with the seal of the *Kohain Gadol*."

"Oil!" everyone took up the cry. "Oil for the holy *Menorah*! Oil to symbolize our holy Torah! Oil to light up for all Yisrael!"

The fighters searched in every corner of the *Bais Hamikdash*. There was oil everywhere; in smashed jars, greasing the floor and staining the walls, smeared on the shields of the Greek soldiers, but not even one sealed jar marked "*Kadosh l'Menorah*" with the seal of the *Kohain Gadol* could be found.

In the afternoon, with the sun dipping and the chill winds howling, everyone grew desperate. One *Kohain* named Kasriel decided to stop searching and recite *Tehillim* that Hashem should help. He wore a long,

long *tallis* with even longer *tzitzis*. He paced back and forth in the oil chamber of the *Bais Hamikdash*, his face buried in his *Tehillim*.

"Just a little bit of oil, just one little jar," he prayed. "Your people want to serve You! Ooops—"

His *tallis* started slipping off, and he grabbed it just in time. His long *tzitzis* had gotten stuck between two stones.

"*Oy, vey!*" he cried. "My *tzitzis* are stuck."

He reached down and tried to pry them up, but they wouldn't budge.

"*Schlemiel* that I am," he sighed. "They're caught on something."

He reached deep down, following the twists of strings as they circled and tangled around something smooth.

Smooth!? What was that?

He felt carefully now, walking his fingers around the neck of a small earthen jar. Could it be? He reached deep, deep down now, and pulled firmly on the jar. It didn't move. But his *tzitzis* were so tangled that he could not free his *tallis* until he pulled out the jar. He yanked and yanked until the small neck of the jar appeared.

Kasriel peered at it closely.

"Why, it's a jar!" he exclaimed. "And it seems to have the seal of the *Kohain Gadol* on it."

Kasriel worked frantically now, tugging harder and harder. His *tzitzis* suddenly slipped free, and then, head first, out came the jar.

Kasriel stared at it in amazement and then gave a shout that reached every corner of the *Bais Hamikdash*.

"Oil!" he cried. "I struck oil!"

Everyone came running.

"Say that again, Kasriel!" they shouted.

"Oil! I've discovered oil," said Kasriel. "Pure oil for the *Menorah*! With the *Kohain Gadol's* seal!"

"*Baruch Hashem*!" the cry rang out joyously. "Oil! Oil! We've found kosher oil!"

Everyone ran to see the one jar of oil that had managed to remain *tahor*, pure. They made a circle around it and kissed it as they would a Torah. Kasriel lifted it high for everyone to see. There was a great celebration.

Meanwhile, inside the jar, the scrawny oil was quietly thanking Hashem.

That night, the old *Kohain Gadol* stood alone in the *Heichal* with the tiny jar of oil. Above him loomed the great, dark *Menorah*.

"Little jar of oil," he whispered. "You are the last pure oil left in all Eretz Yisrael. It will take another week to find new oil, but alas, you just have a little oil in you, just for one night."

He poured the oil into the *Menorah*, lit it and left.

"Hashem," pleaded the oil. "You brought us from the bottom branches of the tree, from the shade of the little *shul* wall in Tekoah, to burn in your *Heichal*. Now we cast our glow in honor of your holy Torah. How can Jews live without Torah? How dare we go out? *Ribono Shel Olam*, please let our light last until new oil is found.

119

Let the holy light of your Torah never be dimmed again. Not even for a second!"

The oil burned ... and burned ... and burned ... and burned ... and burned ... and burned ... and burned ... and burned. And the spirit of its light has not gone out to this very day!

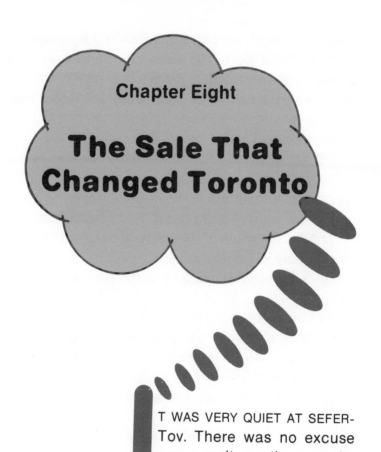

Chapter Eight

The Sale That Changed Toronto

IT WAS VERY QUIET AT SEFER-Tov. There was no excuse anymore. It was three weeks before *Purim,* and the weather was nice. It was just dead quiet.

Rabbi Heller was so nervous that Mrs. Heller came to the store just to keep her husband company. After school, Shulamis and Chaimkel came straight to Sefer-Tov, and even Baruch kept things busy by messing up the shelves. The whole family stood in a row, waiting for customers. But there were none.

Just before closing time at six, Meir the *pushka* man came into the store. His *mitzvah* was to put out *tzedakah* boxes and collect them a few weeks later. His bright smile and humor-filled eyes lightened Rabbi Heller's face.

"*Shalom Aleichem!*" he announced cheerily. "What is this, a family meeting? How are my *pushkas* doing?"

Without waiting for an answer, he went straight to his *pushka* and shook it. His cheerful face fell.

"Why, there's nothing here!" he exclaimed.

"That's the problem," Rabbi Heller sighed. "There is no one here. Business is very slow."

Meir's brow wrinkled, and he tried to console Rabbi Heller.

"Rabbi, everywhere I hear the same thing," he said. "It's not just by you. It's quiet. Very quiet! But don't worry, rabbi. *Pesach* is coming. It'll pick up soon."

"You really think so, Meir?" Rabbi Heller asked.

"I'm telling you, rabbi," Meir insisted. "Now it's all over the same quiet!"

Afterwards, Rabbi Heller drove everyone home in the car. He seemed unusually moody. At dinner, he usually joked with the children or told them some story from the *Midrash*, but now, he seemed very distracted.

"Noach, why are you so glum tonight?" Mrs. Heller asked her husband after dinner. "Is the business getting you down? You mustn't let it. Have *bitachon*! Anyway, we still have a little put away in the bank from the *esrogim* season."

"It's not that," he answered quietly, playing with the

end of a spoon. "Something else is troubling me."

"What?"

"Well," he said. "When Meir mentioned that all the other stores were also doing poorly, for a second I felt happier. But what right do I have to be happy to hear that other people are also struggling? If they are suffering, too, does it make it any better for us?"

"But it's only natural," said Mrs. Heller. "After all, misery loves company."

"That doesn't make it right," he answered. "It's not right, and it's not Jewish. It's not the way a Jew should think. We have to sympathize with the other people who have to make a living as much as ourselves."

"Even *that* store?" interrupted Chaimkel. He didn't want to mention the main competition by name.

Rabbi Heller looked at Chaimkel sharply.

"Especially that store," he said, his voice rising. "We have to *daven* and care especially for them. Otherwise, what does *ve'ohavta l'reyacha kamocha* mean? Just words?"

Chaimkel had rarely seen his father so upset, and he kept out of his way for the rest of the evening.

The next morning, Chaimkel said *Baraich Aleinu*, the *berachah* for *parnassah*, with special *kavanah*. He prayed hard for Sefer-Tov, but he also mentioned the names of a few other stores, even *that* store.

"We must all make a living, Hashem," he whispered.

But things didn't change. Chaimkel even called his father from a pay phone during the school lunch break.

"Is business any better, *Abba*?" he asked.

"No, no change," his father answered lovingly. "Don't worry, Chaimkel. Hashem will help."

"Can I come to the store after school?"

"You have homework, Chaimkel. Also, you are supposed to review your *Mishnayos.*"

"But I want to be with you," Chaimkel pleaded. "I can study in the store. You mustn't be all by yourself when things are so hard."

His father finally gave in. He appreciated Chaimkel's sensitivity.

When Chaimkel left school, it was already dark. He took the bus for the long trip down Bathurst Street to Sefer-Tov. The lights were already on in apartments and stores.

"This is my chance," thought Chaimkel, "to see if the other stores are really doing poorly, like Reb Meir says."

Each store was lit up like a stage. The bus moved slowly and stopped often.

Very soon, they came to Kneidlech, a strictly kosher bakery.

"I wonder if they're also doing terribly," thought Chaimkel as he peered in.

Kneidlech was stuffed. Packed. People were lined up near the shiny glass counters, shouting at the three ladies serving the breads and cakes. People held tickets and waited their turn.

"Things are certainly not quiet at Kneidlech," thought Chaimkel as the bus pulled away.

A few more bus stops and they came to Kishke and

Kigel, the *glatt* kosher butcher shop with the jolly owner.

"They can't be that busy at this time of night, so early in the week," thought Chaimkel.

He looked in. Kigel and Kishke was even more stuffed than Kneidlech. People were reaching into the self-serve shelves and stacking roasts and lampchops in their carts. A few people gathered to watch the liver being broiled, while others gathered around the owner as he came in swinging six fresh new salamis.

"Hmmph," muttered Chaimkel to himself. "Talk about slow business! That Kishke is stuffed from end to end."

The bus moved on. They were getting closer to *that* store—the other Jewish book store that was Sefer-Tov's main competition. The bus slowed down as though the driver understood what Chaimkel wanted. Chaimkel stared in. There was the owner, alone and staring out the window, just like Rabbi Heller. There wasn't a customer in sight. Just like Rabbi Heller, he had rows and rows of beautiful *sefarim* but no customers.

"Why, he's doing just as poorly as we are," sighed Chaimkel. "He needs Hashem's help as much as we do!"

That night, Chaimkel couldn't sleep. He looked up at the ceiling above the bunk-bed he shared with Baruch. Then he turned over and stared into the night outside and the gray light of a street lamp.

Chaimkel thought about all the lovely *sefarim* at Sefer-Tov and that store. It wasn't fair. The new books were so beautiful, with brown, maroon and black covers, etched with gold lettering. The English *sefarim* were colorfully decorated, and the explanations inside were clear.

The *sefarim* were so wonderful! Why weren't there more customers?

In his mind, he marched his fingers from cover to cover, studying each letter, flipping through the pages. He opened the pages of a *Minchas Chinuch*, the *sefer* that explained all six hundred and thirteen commandments. In the middle, like a great etched window, were the words of the *Chinuch* and all around, like a frame, the letters of the *Minchas Chinuch*.

He opened the window and climbed in. He was in a vast room with thousands of *sefarim* stacked high on the shelves. Row after row, bookshelf after bookshelf.

"Where did all these *sefarim* come from?" he wondered. "There are thousands more than just at Sefer-Tov."

He studied them more closely and then jumped back in shock. Why, these were the *sefarim* of Sefer-Tov and that other store combined! They must have all joined together for a meeting. He hid behind a glass counter and carefully watched the proceedings.

The *sefarim* of each store were facing each other. On one end was a great twenty-volume *Shass* with bright yellow covers. It spoke first, with a great rumbling voice like the thunder of waves.

"*Rabbosai*, what is going on here?" roared the *Shass*. "Look at me! Twenty volumes of Hashem's *Torah She-b'al Peh*. In me you can find every *Mishneh*. Through me you can understand *Halachah*. In me you can find beautiful parables and *Mussar*. But who runs after me?"

"You can say that again," responded the *Noam Elimelech* politely. "Here, look at my appendix. Do you see what I have?" All the *sefarim* tipped on their sides to get a closer look. "You see, I contain, the *Tzetel Katan* of Reb Elimelech of Lizhensk. Look how it begins. If a Jew has free time, he should concentrate on how he is ready at any moment to give up his life *al Kiddush Hashem*, to sacrifice himself for the honor of Hashem. How many people review me daily, do you think?"

The *sefarim* all rustled their heads sadly.

"I bet I know a set that must be doing well," said a thick, red bound volume of the *Tur*, pointing to the *Mishneh Berurah*. "Your *Halachos* are all so clearly outlined and brought up to date. I see how set after set of you is pulled off the shelf and given as a *Bar Mitzvah* gift. At least you must be doing well."

"*Baruch Hashem*, not to complain," answered the *Mishneh Berurah* politely. "But not everything is the way it appears. One of my volumes was exchanged the other week because of a misprint, and he gave me a disturbing report."

"How so?" asked the *Shulchan Aruch*.

"He said that he'd been on the shelf of the house for

a few weeks, and . . ." The *Mishneh Berurah* paused.

"And, what?" asked the *Shulchan Aruch*.

"Well, that was it," said the *Mishneh Berurah*. "Nothing. It was put on the shelf and that's that. What good is a *Mishneh Berurah* that's not opened every day, if only to study a few *Halachos* before bed time?"

"I agree," spoke up the blue covered set of *Torah Temimah*. "Too many *sefarim* are left to collect dust."

A great silence fell on the room. Chaimkel shifted nervously from leg to leg. It was as if all the holy *sefarim* were deep in thought, trying to figure out how people could be made to study them.

Finally, in words spoken so quietly and humbly that they could hardly be heard, the thin volume of *Mesillas Yesharim* spoke up.

"My precious *sefarim*," said the *Mesillas Yesharim*. "May I make a suggestion with your permission?"

"Please," said the *Shass* in his rumbling voice.

"If we want people to buy more *sefarim* and study more Torah, we must teach them to learn the right way."

"What do you mean?" asked the *Noam Elimelech*.

"People mustn't buy *sefarim* just to sit on their book shelves," said the *Mesillas Yesharim*.

"You mean they should study what they buy," said the *Mishneh Berurah*.

"Yes," said the *Mesillas Yesharim*. "But even that is not enough. When a Jew studies, it is not just so that he can repeat it or show it off to others. It has to be *Torah l'Shemah*, for its own sake, to fulfill the Will of Hashem."

"Oh, if we could only get everyone to study like that," glowed the *Aish Das*, "what a bright world it would be."

"*Rabbosai*," the great black-covered *Rambam*, with its great gold letters, spoke up for the first time. "Even that is not enough. Things must start here at the very source!"

"What do you mean by that? Explain yourself!" demanded the *Raavad*.

"Look at us *sefarim* here," said the *Rambam*. "Here is a *Rambam* from Sefer-Tov, and there is a *Rambam* from the other store. Here is a *Shass* from there and a *Shass* from here. *Mishneh Berurahs* and *Mikraos Gedolos* and all the wonderful *sefarim* that teach Hashem's Torah are in every store."

"So? So?" asked the *Raavad* impatiently.

"So doesn't it teach *ve'ohavta l'reyacha kamocha*? That one must love one's fellow Jew like oneself? The booksellers themselves must show that they are selling not just for business but also for the *mitzvah*. They must help each other and rejoice in each other's success. In this way, all Jews will be inspired."

"But who will tell this to the booksellers?" asked the *Pnai Yehoshua*.

There was a momentary silence, and the *sefarim* stared at each other. Chaimkel was unable to contain himself. He jumped up from his hiding place.

"*Sefarim, sefarim!*" he cried. "Here I am! I will tell what you said to my *Abba*, and even to the other store. Do you hear?"

But there was only silence. The *sefarim* stood

stacked like canyon walls on either side of the aisle, gazing down at him. Chaimkel raced down the aisle, turning from one *sefer* to the next.

"*Sefarim, sefarim,*" he cried. "Please talk to me! Let me try!"

He grabbed a shelf and started shaking it.

"Answer me! Please answer me!"

He shook harder, until the whole store started to shake. The books were beginning to fall.

"Chaimkel! Chaimkel!" a voice shouted back.

"Oh yes, *Pnai Yehoshua,*" said Chaimkel. "Tell me."

"*Pnai Yehoshua*? *Pnai Yehoshua*?" said Rabbi Heller. "It's just me, your *Abba.*"

Chaimkel popped open an eye. "Huh?" he said. "I thought you were the *Pnai Yehoshua.* And where's the *Mesillas Yesharim*?"

Rabbi Heller laughed.

"Chaimkel, you and your dreams again," he said.

Later that morning, Chaimkel got up the nerve to approach his father.

"*Abba,*" he said. "I have an idea."

"I know, Chaimkel," said Rabbi Heller. "Used books."

"No, but let's have a sale."

"A sale? What kind of sale?" asked Rabbi Heller suspiciously.

"A *Torah l'Shemah* sale!"

"Hmm," mused Rabbi Heller. "An interesting idea. How did you think of it?"

"Just dreamed it up," said Chaimkel.

The next evening, the floor of the Heller living room

was covered with blank posters. Chaimkel and Shulamis blocked in large, square letters in black magic markers and later colored them in.

SALE!!! SALE!!!
Come to the *Torah l'Shemah* Sale!
Come and buy *sefarim*
and
study our holy Torah
***l'Shemah*!!!!!**

They worked as a team. In a short while, almost a dozen posters were ready. Rabbi Heller came over to admire the signs.

"They're beautiful," he decided. "They will inspire everyone."

"I bet that other store will wish he'd thought of the idea first," said Shulamis.

Just then, Chaimkel remembered the rest of his dream. Jumping up from the posters, he turned to his father.

"*Abba*, wouldn't it be nice if we had our sale together with that other store?" he said. "What if we told people that it didn't matter where they bought their *sefarim*, as long as they studied *Torah l'Shemah*?"

"That's a beautiful idea," chimed in Mrs. Heller.

"Chaimkel, where do you come up with these ideas?"
But Rabbi Heller frowned.

"There's one big problem," he said. "Since I've been in Toronto, I've never spoken to the owner of that other store. If I call him, he may think that . . ."

"That what?" pressed Chaimkel.

"That it sounds suspicious," said Rabbi Heller. "That we're trying to pull something."

"*Abba*, isn't he also a *Shomer Shabbos*?" persisted Chaimkel. "Doesn't he study Torah? Doesn't he also learn about the *mitzvah* of *Torah l'Shemah*? Maybe he'll agree. Oh, *Abba*, can't you call him?"

"Please, *Abba*!" pressed Shulamis. "Call him!"
Rabbi Heller looked to his wife. She nodded.

"If it is a real *Torah l'Shemah* sale," she said, "then everyone should be included. Not just us."

Hesitantly, Rabbi Heller went to his study and began dialing. The family waited breathlessly near the door, trying to hear what was happening. Rabbi Heller stood up and shut the door.

Ten minutes passed. Fifteen minutes. Twenty minutes. Almost a half hour.

Finally, Rabbi Heller opened his study door. The family was shocked. Rabbi Heller's eyes were red rimmed. Chaimkel could tell he'd been crying. For a moment, Chaimkel was full of regret. Had he caused his father embarrassment?

"What happened, Noach?" asked Mrs. Heller.
Rabbi Heller sat down.

"As soon as I called that store the owner came to the

phone," he said. "I think he was as surprised and nervous as I was. We spoke some small talk, and then I jumped right in and asked him if we could get together and make a *Torah l'Shemah* sale."

"And then?" pressed Mrs. Heller. Chaimkel's heart almost stopped.

"Then, he just burst into tears," said Rabbi Heller.

"What!?" exclaimed everyone.

"Yes," said Rabbi Heller, his voice getting shaky. "He actually started crying like a baby. Finally, he got control of himself and told me his problem. He is doing as poorly as we are. He thought we were doing great, but I set him straight on that. He thought it was a beautiful idea. He loves *sefarim* as much as we do. He sent a special *berachah* to whomever had the idea!"

All eyes turned to Chaimkel.

The next Sunday, Toronto saw something it had never seen before. On every store wall and lamp post were signs that read as follows:

★ ★ ★ ★ ★
**IT DOESN'T MATTER
WHERE YOU BUY
IT DOESN'T MATTER
LOW OR HIGH
BUY *SEFARIM* GALORE
LEARN *TORAH L'SHEMAH*
MORE AND MORE!!!!**
★ ★ ★ ★ ★

The names of Sefer-Tov and the other book store were etched at the bottom of each poster.

The idea struck Toronto like a thunderbolt. No one had ever heard of two competing stores working to help each other. People felt it wasn't just another sale. The city was hit by a wave, a Torah and *mitzvah* wave.

And it worked incredibly well. Suddenly, people who had been lukewarm about learning streamed into Sefer-Tov and the other store. New *shiurim* and lecture series were begun. More *Baalei Teshuvah* knocked on the doors of the *shuls*.

It was not just study. It was not just Torah. It was *Torah l'Shemah*!

Rabbi Heller couldn't believe his eyes or his cash register. It was unbelievable. From the day the *Torah l'Shemah* sale started, Sefer-Tov and the other store got busier and busier. Rabbi Heller stopped worrying so much about *parnassah*. He was able to study more Torah. He stopped reading the classified sections of the Jewish newspapers to see if there were any rabbinical posts open.

On his eleventh birthday, Chaimkel was presented with a specially bound edition of the *Mesillas Yesharim* by his father and the owner of the other store. It was inscribed as follows: To the boy who changed Toronto!

That night, Chaimkel had a sweet dream. He was swept out of his bed and lifted up into the blue sky, carried past golden sunbeams and fluffy white clouds, and set down on a long, winding road. Birds sang from the trees, and butterflies darted overhead.

On both sides of the road, there were hundreds of open *sefarim*, their white pages flapping like wings. There were *Chumashim, Gemaras, Rishonim, Acharonim, Mussar* and *Chassidus.* The letters of each page stood out black and clear, ready to read.

"Study me! Study me!" the pages whispered to Chaimkel. "Learn our holy words!"

"Torah, Torah, I will!" Chaimkel called out into the wind. "I'll study every one of your pages."

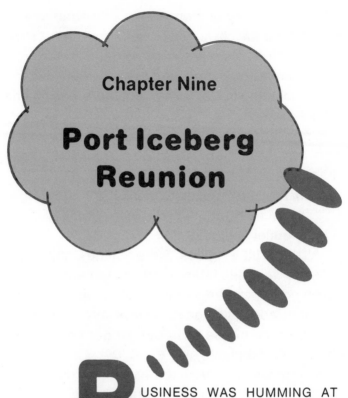

Chapter Nine

Port Iceberg Reunion

BUSINESS WAS HUMMING AT Sefer-Tov. The store had expanded, and new customers came in every day. People from as far away as Calgary, Edmonton and Rochester came in to buy kosher *mezuzos* and *tefillin*. A year after the famous *Torah l'Shemah* sale, the Hellers put a down-payment on a small house.

Two weeks after *Pesach*, when things usually slowed to a trickle, the store suddenly became very busy. People never seen before started coming into the store, and many of them spoke with strange accents.

"*Shalom aleichem*, y'all," said one man. "How y'all doin' today?"

Chaimkel looked around to see whom else the man was including in his "y'alls," but there was no one else in the store.

Soon, another man came in.

"I say, old chap," he said to Chaimkel. "You don't happen to have a *Kol Eliyhahu*, do you?"

"*Kol Eliyahu*?" asked Chaimkel, trying to remember.

"Yes, quite right," said the man. "*Kol Eliyahu*. Quite. Quite, quite! Quite right!"

All those little "quites" were getting Chaimkel jumpy.

A few minutes later, another man entered. He also seemed to have something wrong with his speech.

"Say, laddie, you have *sefarim*, ay?" asked the man. "Some nice hoose of books ya got here, some nice hoose. Good place, ay?"

The three men browsed happily through the store, throwing out "y'alls" and "quites" and "ays" at each other up and down the aisles. Why are they all talking so strangely? wondered Chaimkel.

In a few minutes, his father returned from *davening Minchah*. He noticed all the men in the store and greeted them warmly. They were all enjoying the beautiful *sefarim*, making large stacks of what they wanted to purchase.

Chaimkel pulled his father into the back office.

"*Abba*," he said. "Why do they all talk so strangely?"

Rabbi Heller laughed.

"Chaimkel, you haven't been around much, have you?" he said. "These men obviously come from different parts of the world. The 'y'all' man comes from the American South. The 'quite! quite!' man must be a Britisher. While the 'hoose' and 'ay' man may be from the Maritime Provinces, perhaps Newfoundland."

Chaimkel pondered his father's explanation. "A Jew from Newfoundland," he mused. "Is that like a Galitzianer?"

Even while they spoke, the store door opened yet again, and more people piled in.

"What's going on here, *Abba*?" asked Chaimkel. "It's late in the afternoon, in the middle of the week. Why are there so many people here?"

Rabbi Heller went out to investigate. Many of the men seemed to recognize each other.

"*Rabbosai!*" greeted Rabbi Heller. "It is a pleasure to have you all here this afternoon. But I am curious. Is there a special reason you are all in Toronto today?"

They all looked at him, slightly dumfounded.

"I am surprised you don't know," said a short man with a long shock of white hair.

"Know? Know what?" asked Rabbi Heller.

"Why, there's a big convention in town," said the man with the white hair. "A rabbinical convention from all over North America. All of us here are rabbis who've come to the convention."

"What's a rabbinical convention?" asked Chaimkel.

One of the rabbis with an unlit pipe dangling in his mouth laughed.

"That's when all the rabbis from the States and Canada come to discuss their problems," he said. "There are hundreds of us gathered at the Union Hotel."

Another rabbi, a younger man, congratulated Rabbi Heller.

"You are lucky to have such a book store," he commented. "Back in the Kentucky town I come from you don't have this many *sefarim* in the whole city!"

"You ought to see New Mexico," responded yet another.

The rabbis retired to a corner of the store to discuss their congregations and memories. Rabbi Heller went back to pricing *sefarim*, and Chaimkel set them on the shelves. There was such a hubbub they did not hear the latest customer come in.

"Harumph," said a voice that sounded somewhat familiar. "Rabbi Heller, I believe."

Rabbi Heller and Chaimkel looked up. Rabbi Heller's mouth fell open. Why, it couldn't be! But it was. There stood Mr. Goldenberg, the *gabbai* from Port Iceberg! For a split second, Rabbi Heller's knees trembled, until he remembered that it was *his* store and that Mr. Goldenberg was just another customer. Rabbi Heller extended his hand in greeting.

"Mr. Goldenberg, is it you?" asked Rabbi Heller. "*Shalom aleichem!*"

Mr. Goldenberg coughed impatiently and returned the hand-shake weakly.

"Of course, it's me," he said. "Who else would I be? I heard you bought a book store here in Toronto. Funny,

141

I never figured you for a businessman. I thought rabbis were supposed to be more spiritual. Harumph!"

"What brings you down to Toronto?" asked Rabbi Heller.

"Well," confided Mr. Goldenberg. "The truth is that Port Iceberg is looking for a new rabbi."

"A new rabbi?" wondered Rabbi Heller. "I thought you just got a new rabbi six months ago."

"We did," answered Mr. Goldenberg impatiently. "But there was a bit of a mix-up. We were very disappointed. We didn't like the way the rabbi dressed. What do you call those little curls that grow around the ears?"

"*Peyos.*"

"Whatever," said Mr. Goldenberg. "Too extreme for our town. We had to let him go."

"Tsk, tsk." Rabbi Heller shook his head. "Just six months. But what brings you here now?"

"I heard there was a convention of rabbis in Toronto," said Mr. Goldenberg. "I thought it would be a good place to go fishing for a rabbi. There must be someone who needs a new job."

Chaimkel stood there quietly, listening to the conversation. He could hardly control himself. The blood rushed to his face. Another rabbi! He remembered how his poor father had trembled before this man and how this man had sent his father away from Port Iceberg with hardly enough money to buy Baruch a cookie.

Rabbi Heller noticed Chaimkel's flushed face, and

he understood immediately. He gave Chaimkel a sharp, no-nonsense look.

"Chaimkel," he suddenly remembered. "We have a package of *mezuzos* to deliver to the Wohls. Why don't you bring it over? Now."

"But, *Abba*," protested Chaimkel.

"Right now, Chaimkel," his father said softly, but very, very firmly. "Right now. Go!"

Still fuming, Chaimkel grabbed the package of *mezuzos*. But not without one final angry glance at Mr. Goldenberg.

That night, Chaimkel tossed and turned in bed. Sleep wouldn't come. Mr. Goldenberg's sudden appearance had brought back so many memories. The dark, gray afternoon when he had pleaded with the Torah, the snowbound night at Congregation Anshei Iceberg, his encounter with the ghost-white *minyan* and many more.

Sefer-Tov had been such a hard struggle, scratching dollar to dollar, penny to penny. How his father had worried, suffered and even cried to make the little bookstore survive! He was so angry at Mr. Goldenberg, the man who had made life so hard for his family.

Suddenly, Chaimkel caught himself. How was he allowed to be angry at a fellow Jew? No, he would overcome his anger. He would make himself think pleasant thoughts.

He closed his eyes, lay back dreamily and let his mind float back to Sefer-Tov, lined top to bottom with deep red, brown and gold-stamped *sefarim*. The store was crowded with customers, interesting rabbis from all over the world who walked happily about, flipping through the volumes, choosing huge piles of *sefarim* to purchase.

And there was Mr. Goldenberg, standing before his father like a pupil before his rabbi.

Rabbi Heller beamed happily and banged on the glass counter for attention.

"*Rabbosai*! Fellow rabbis!" he announced. "I have the honor of introducing you to Mr. Goldenberg of Port Iceberg, Canada. His *shul* is looking for a new rabbi!"

"Just one minute!" bellowed a voice from the corner of the store.

Rabbi Heller looked up. It was the rabbi with the long shock of white hair. He was racing down the aisle to them, anger in his eyes.

"Is that Joe Goldenberg from Port Iceberg?" he demanded.

Mr. Goldenberg turned around quickly.

"Why, yes," he said. "Who are you?"

The white haired rabbi moved closer.

"Don't you remember me?" he asked. "Rabbi David Friedman from Minnesota who served as your rabbi twenty years ago."

Mr. Goldenberg looked surprised.

"You're Rabbi Friedman?" he said. "I didn't recognize you. You've turned all white."

"Say, y'all," interrupted the rabbi from the American South. "Y'all recognize me from 1978, Mr. Goldenberg? I'm Asher Bergman. I was rabbi in Port Iceberg for two years. Grits and glitz! It took us all of six years in Houston to defrost."

"Why, Rabbi Bergman, are you here also?" said Mr. Goldenberg. "Why do you talk so funny now?"

"You certainly remember me, ay, Mr. Goldenberg?" asked the rabbi from Newfoundland. "Sam Katz. You gave me exactly seventy-two hours to leave Port Iceberg, ay?"

"Why, Rabbi Katz!" exclaimed Mr. Goldenberg, becoming quite flustered. "Are you here, too?"

"I say!" said the British rabbi. "You jolly well remember me, Mr. Goldenberg, old chap, don't you? Mordechai Steiner. My first post in the Colonies was in Port Iceberg. I was there one year before you sent me packing."

"And how about me, Mr. Goldenberg?" said the rabbi who sucked on the unlit pipe. "You must remember me. Barry Blitz. Now let's see. When did you chase me out of Port Iceberg? How long ago was that? Kinda hard to remember. Two years in Wyoming. Six years in Wichita. Four years in Nebraska. Now, let's see . . ."

All the rabbis crowded around Mr. Goldenberg who had begun to perspire heavily. He looked to Rabbi Heller for protection, but Chaimkel's father was too busy pricing *sefarim* to look up.

"Well, it's been a pleasure, gentleman," said Mr. Goldenberg and turned to leave.

"Wait a second!" ordered the white-haired Rabbi. "You're not going anywhere, Joe Goldenberg. Do you know what we have here?"

"Here?" asked Mr. Goldenberg nervously. "Where?"

"Here!" answered the white-haired rabbi sharply. "Look around. You have here far more than three rabbis. Do you know what three rabbis are? They're a *Bais Din*, a rabbinical court. Lock the door, gentlemen! We are going to convene a *Bais Din* and call Mr. Goldenberg to a *Din Torah*."

"I'm getting out of here," said Mr. Goldenberg nervously. He picked up his gloves from the counter.

Rabbi Heller placed his hand gently on Mr. Goldenberg's shoulder.

"When a *Bais Din* summons you, you must not refuse," he said softly.

Mr. Goldenberg looked at the locked door and the crowd of rabbis.

"Oh, okay," he said unwillingly. "If I must. But make it quick. I have a six o'clock appointment, rabbis or no rabbis!"

Rabbi Heller set up three chairs on the crowded floor for the *Bais Din* and one for Mr. Goldenberg.

"What do you guys want from me?" demanded Mr. Goldenberg in his angry, nasal voice. "I never did you anything wrong. Why, I paid each of you a good salary when you were in Port Iceberg. I dare you to deny it!"

"I accuse you in front of the *Bais Din*," said the white-haired rabbi.

"Accuse me? Of what?"

"I was a young rabbi when I came to Port Iceberg," began the white-haired rabbi. "I was young and quite

146

idealistic. You finished that. I've kept tabs on your community. You've had twenty-two rabbis in twenty-nine years."

"Twenty-one!" retorted Mr. Goldenberg.

"Twenty-two," insisted the white-haired rabbi. "You fired Izzy Nussbaum twice. You have never let a rabbi live in peace in your community. You've hounded them out every time."

"It wasn't me," said Mr. Goldenberg. "There was a whole board."

"It was you with everyone else," said the rabbi. "You never respected your rabbis. You never listened to them."

"They were all strange," said Mr. Goldenberg. "They didn't fit in."

"Really? And how were they strange? Were they strange because they came to teach Torah and keeping *Shabbos*? Because they came to teach you to sanctify your homes? Because they came to teach you to open your homes to the poor? They came to change you! They came to uplift you! But would you listen? No-o-o!"

"No-o-o!!" cried the *Bais Din* together.

"Why did all twenty-two rabbis make such sacrifices to come to Port Iceberg?" continued the white-haired rabbi. "Weren't they smart enough to become doctors, lawyers, computer operators or businessmen? They were! Look at Rabbi Heller here! Look how well he's doing! Why did these rabbis go to Port Iceberg? Why do they go to Utah, Texas, California, New

Hampshire or Saskatoon? They go because they love Hashem and they love people. Because they want to draw the Jewish people back to their roots. But would you listen? No-o-o!!"

"No-o-o!!" shouted the court.

"What did they find when they came with their wives and children into faraway Port Iceberg?" continued the white-haired rabbi. "Were they made the shining example to follow? Or fish in the bowl to be stared at and complained about? Was there any consideration, any caring? No-o-o!!"

"No-o-o!!" screamed the court, staring angrily at him.

"And you, Mr. Goldenberg, the *gabbai*," said the white-haired rabbi, his voice rising sharply. "Did you ever come out and challenge the rabbi man to man? No! Always issuing your own decisions through a meeting, a board committee. Always ten against one. Never opening a *Shulchan Aruch* to see what Jewish law demands. And have you changed in all these years? No-o-o!!"

"No-o-o!!" chanted the court. "No-o-o!! No-o-o!! Never! Never!!"

"*Rabbosai* of the *Bais Din*," thundered the white-haired rabbi. "I demand a judgment against Mr. Goldenberg, a judgment that will make up for all the past injustices."

"What do you mean?" asked the court.

"I demand that as punishment and atonement for the suffering, embarrassment and injustice suffered by all twenty-two past rabbis of Port Iceberg, the next rabbi hired by Port Iceberg should be kept on for life."

"Now wait a second!" shouted Mr. Goldenberg, his face turning red. "That's too much to ask."

"No, it is not!" shouted the white-haired rabbi. "The *Bais Din* must insist that the new rabbi be kept on and that the congregation obey the rabbi's decisions."

Mr. Goldenberg was beside himself.

"But that's unbelievable!" he screeched. "No congregation has to listen to its rabbi."

"Furthermore," persisted the white-haired rabbi. "The congregation must show respect to its rabbi. Everyone must stand up when the rabbi enters, attend his lectures and follow the rabbi's teachings."

"That's not fair!" cried Mr. Goldenberg desperately. "No congregation has to listen to the rabbi. Why should Port Iceberg have to suffer?"

But it was too late. The Beth Din was already conferring among themselves. Mr. Goldenberg was trapped. Chaimkel couldn't make out the words, but there were a lot of "y'alls" and "jolly good ideas" and "ays" coming from the huddle. Finally, the *Bais Din* was ready. One of them stood up.

"It is our decision," he began, "that the next rabbi you hire must be kept for life. And he must be shown respect. And you must listen to his decision. If not, Mr. Goldenberg, you will be held personally responsible."

"But—" Mr. Goldenberg began to protest.

"Y'all didn't hear straight?" yelled the rabbi from the American South. "It is the judgment of this *Bais Din*!"

Mr. Goldenberg looked to Rabbi Heller anxiously. After all, it was his store.

"You'd better listen, Mr. Goldenberg," Rabbi Heller said quietly.

Stunned, Mr. Goldenberg grabbed his gloves, pulled on his hat and ran off. He slammed the door behind him so hard that the store began to shake. Suddenly, it began to shake so hard that it looked as if all the *sefarim* in Sefer-Tov would fall from the shelves. All the rabbis ran for the door. Chaimkel grabbed the counter to stop himself from falling to the ground.

"Chaimkel, Chaimkel," said Rabbi Heller as he shook his shoulder. "It's time to get up and go to school."

Chaimkel's eyes came open. He was relieved to see that he was safe in his room.

That afternoon, when Chaimkel came to the store, it was even more crowded than on the previous day. Rabbis and more rabbis filled every aisle. Towards the end of the day, the door opened and Mr. Goldenberg came in.

"Good afternoon, Rabbi Heller," he said. "You'll be happy to know we've found a new rabbi for Port Iceberg."

"I am very happy for you," said Rabbi Heller. "Was it hard?"

Mr. Goldenberg fidgeted a little.

"Well, it wasn't easy," he said. "We had to make him some special offers."

"What kind of offers?" asked Rabbi Heller.

"Well, we had to offer him a lifetime contract," said Mr. Goldenberg. "And a few other conditions. But we really had no choice."

Rabbi Heller smiled. "I'm sure you didn't, Mr. Goldenberg," he said.

A few minutes later, all the rabbis tallied their books and left to return to their convention. Rabbi Heller and Chaimkel got ready to close up. As they locked the front door, Chaimkel turned to his father.

"It was a good day for Sefer-Tov, wasn't it, *Abba*?"

Their eyes met.

"Yes," answered Rabbi Heller. "And an even greater day for Port Iceberg."

Glossary

GLOSSARY

Abba: father, daddy

al Kiddush Hashem: to sanctify the Name

aliyah: honorary post at the Torah reading

arav(ah)(os): willow branch(es)

Aron Hakodesh: the Holy Ark of the Torah

baal habayis (baalei batim): owner(s)

Baal(ei) Teshuvah: penitent(s)

Bais Medrash: study hall

Bais Din: rabbinical court

Bais Hamikdash: the Holy Temple

bais: second letter of the Hebrew alphabet

Bar Mitzvah: Halachic coming of age

Baruch Hashem: blessed is the Name

berachah: blessing

Beraishis: in the beginning

bimah: platform

bitachon: trust

bli neder: without making an oath

bubba's bubba: grandmother's grandmother [Yiddish]

Chanukah: Festival of Lights

Chassidus: Chassidic philosophy

chazan: cantor

chulent: special Sabbath stew

Chumash: (Five) Book(s) of Moses

D'var Torah: Torah thought

Daf Yomi: daily *Talmud* study

daven(ed)(ing): pray(ed)(ing)

Din Torah: *Halachic* litigation

esrog(im): citron(s)

Gabbai: beadle of the congregation

Gabbai Sheni: assistant beadle

Gam zu l'tovah: this too is for the good

Gemara: volume of the *Talmud*

giddel: sloping top

Gizbar: custodian

glatt: strictly

Halachah: Torah law

Imma: mother, mommy

Kadosh l'Menorah: sanctified for the *Menorah*

kaporah: atonement

kavanah: concentration

Kiddush: ritual sanctification of the Sabbath

Kohain: priest

Kohain Gadol: high priest

latke(s): pancake(s)

Levi: Levite

Litvishe Yiddish: Lithuanian Yiddish dialect [Yiddish]

lulav: palm leaf

Machzor(im): festival prayer book(s)
Makom Torah: Torah center
maven: expert
mazel: good fortune
mechitza: partition
mehudar: beautiful
Menorah: candelabrum
mezuzos: scrolls for doorposts
Minchah: afternoon service
minyan: quorum of ten
mitzvah: commandment
Mussar: Torah ethics
Ner Tamid: eternal flame
neshamos: souls
niggun: melody
Oy, vey: lamentation [Yiddish]
Oy, gevalt: lamentation [Yiddish]
parnassah: livelihood
parnassah tovah: bountiful livelihood
Parshah: weekly portion
Pesach: Festival of Passover
pesukim: verses from the Torah
peyos: earlocks
pitum: knobby protrusion at top of *esrog*
posul: not valid
Purim: Festival of Lots
pushka: collection box
rabbosai: gentlemen
Ribono Shel Olam: Master of the Universe
schlemiel: silly fool

sefer (sefarim): book(s)
Sefer (Sifrei) Torah: Torah scroll(s)
sha-shtill: utter silence [Yiddish]
Shabbos: the Sabbath
Shacharis: morning services
Shalom: peace
Shalom aleichem: greetings
shammas: synagogue attendant
Shavuos: Festival of Weeks
shaymess: scraps of holy books
sheiner: handsome
Shema: daily prayer
shidduchim: matrimonial matches
Shinui Hashem: change of name
shiur(im): lecture(s)
Shomer Shabbos: Sabbath observer
shtender: student's lectern
shul: synagogue
Shulchan Aruch: Code of Jewish Law
Siddur(im): prayer book(s)
Sukkos: Festival of Tabernacles
tahor: pure
tall(is)(eisim): prayer shawl(s)
Talmid Chacham: Torah scholar
tamai: contaminated
Tanach: the Written Torah

tefillin: phylacteries
Tehillim: Book of Psalms
Torah l'Shemah: Torah for its own sake
Torah Sheb'al Peh: the Oral Torah
tzedakah: charity
Tzetel Katan: short list
tzitzis: fringes
v'ohavta l'reyacha kamocha: love your fellow as yourself

Yahrzeit: date of passing
yarmulke: skullcap
Yasher koach: thank you
yeshiv(ah)(os): Torah academies
yingelle: little boy [Yiddish]
Yiras Shamayim: fear of Heaven
Yom Tov: Festival